200 HARLEY STREET

Welcome to the luxurious premises of
the exclusive Hunter Clinic, world renowned
in plastic and reconstructive surgery,
set right on Harley Street, the centre of
elite clinical excellence, in the heart of
London's glittering West End!

Owned by two very different brothers,
Leo and Ethan Hunter, the Hunter Clinic
undertakes both cosmetic and reconstructive
surgery. Playboy Leo handles the rich and
famous clients, enjoying the red carpet
glamour of London's A-list social scene,
while brooding ex-army doc Ethan
focuses his time on his passion—
transforming the lives of injured war heroes
and civilian casualties of war.

Emotion and drama abound against the
backdrop of one of Europe's most glamorous
cities, as Leo and Ethan work
through their tensions and find women
who will change their lives for ever!

200 HARLEY STREET

*Glamour, intensity, desire—the lives and loves
of London's hottest team of surgeons!*

Dear Reader

When I was invited to take part in the *200 Harley Street* continuity I was absolutely thrilled—not only because this is my first ever Mills & Boon® Medical Romance™ continuity contribution, but because it also meant I got the chance to work closely with some amazing authors and some very interesting plotlines. So a big thank you to everyone for taking a newbie under your collective wings!

Declan Underwood and Kara Stephens come from two very different worlds, but both have fled to London to start new lives in their chosen field of Burns and Plastic Medicine. Falling in love is definitely not on the cards for either of them, so it's very inconvenient when a mutual attraction starts to sizzle!

Australian Kara was a joy to write: she's funny and confident and shares my love of shoes. Like many of us, she'll live with pain in exchange for a decent heel and the softest of soft suede! But she also has a history of choosing the wrong men, so staying away from Declan is her preferred course of action.

But who can resist a bad-boy Irishman? Farmboy Declan, with his smoulderingly good looks and an accent that purrs as sexily as his motorbike, has no intention of getting involved with Kara; his life is already too full of commitments to his career and providing for his mother and four sisters. But that's where I come in: plotting ways of getting them together even when they don't want to be anywhere near each other…

I hope you enjoy reading this book as much as I enjoyed writing it.

Drop me a line at louisageorgeauthor@gmail.com or visit me at www.louisageorge.com

Happy reading!

Louisa x

Recent titles by Louisa George:

HOW TO RESIST A HEARTBREAKER*
THE LAST DOCTOR SHE SHOULD EVER DATE
THE WAR HERO'S LOCKED AWAY HEART
WAKING UP WITH HIS RUNAWAY BRIDE
ONE MONTH TO BECOME A MUM

*The Infamous Maitland Brothers

200 HARLEY STREET: THE SHAMELESS MAVERICK

BY
LOUISA GEORGE

First published in Great Britain 2014
by Mills & Boon, an imprint of Harlequin (UK) Limited,
Large Print edition 2015
Eton House, 18-24 Paradise Road,
Richmond, Surrey, TW9 1SR

© 2014 Harlequin Books S.A.

Special thanks and acknowledgement are given to
Louisa George for her contribution to the
200 Harley Street series

ISBN: 978-0-263-25450-1

Printed and bound in Great Britain
by CPI Antony Rowe, Chippenham, Wiltshire

A lifelong reader of most genres, **Louisa George** discovered romance novels later than most, but immediately fell in love with the intensity of emotion, the high drama and the family focus of Mills & Boon® Medical Romance™.

With a Bachelors Degree in Communication and a nursing qualification under her belt, writing medical romance seemed a natural progression and the perfect combination of her two interests. And making things up is a great way to spend the day!

An English ex-pat, Louisa now lives north of Auckland, New Zealand, with her husband, two teenage sons and two male cats. Writing romance is her opportunity to covertly inject a hefty dose of pink into her heavily testosterone-dominated household. When she's not writing or researching Louisa loves to spend time with her family and friends, enjoys travelling and adores great food. She's also hopelessly addicted to Zumba®.

Dedication

To Kamy Chetty, thanks for all your support, positive words and help with the icky medical details (any errors are totally mine). xx

And to Jane Beckenham, without you I just wouldn't be here, writing this—thank you so much for all your support, enthusiasm and words of wisdom and for introducing me to the world of romance books…this one's for you! xx

200 HARLEY STREET

*Glamour, intensity, desire—the lives and loves of
London's hottest team of surgeons!*

**For the next four months enter the world of London's
elite surgeons as they transform the lives of their patients
and find love amidst a sea of passions and tensions…!**

Renowned plastic surgeon and legendary playboy
Leo Hunter can't resist the challenge of unbuttoning
the intriguing new head nurse, Lizzie Birch!
200 HARLEY STREET: SURGEON IN A TUX
by Carol Marinelli

Glamorous Head of PR Lexi Robbins is determined
to make gruff, grieving and super-sexy Scottish surgeon Iain MacKenzie
her Hunter Clinic star!
200 HARLEY STREET: GIRL FROM THE RED CARPET
by Scarlet Wilson

Top-notch surgeons and estranged spouses
Rafael and Abbie de Luca find being forced to work together again
tough as their passion is as incendiary as ever!
200 HARLEY STREET: THE PROUD ITALIAN
by Alison Roberts

One night with his new colleague, surgeon Grace Turner, sees
former Hollywood plastic surgeon Mitchell Cooper daring to live again…
200 HARLEY STREET: AMERICAN SURGEON IN LONDON
by Lynne Marshall

Injured war hero Prince Marco meets physical therapist
Becca Anderson—the woman he once shared a magical *forbidden*
summer romance with long ago…
200 HARLEY STREET: THE SOLDIER PRINCE
by Kate Hardy

When genius micro-surgeon Edward North meets single mum
Nurse Charlotte King she opens his eyes to a whole new world…
200 HARLEY STREET: THE ENIGMATIC SURGEON
by Annie Claydon

Junior surgeon Kara must work with hot-shot
Irish surgeon Declan Underwood—the man she kissed at the hospital ball!
200 HARLEY STREET: THE SHAMELESS MAVERICK
by Louisa George

Brilliant charity surgeon Olivia Fairchild faces the man who once
broke her heart—damaged ex-soldier Ethan Hunter. Yet she's unprepared
for his haunted eyes and the shock of his sensual touch…!
200 HARLEY STREET: THE TORTURED HERO by Amy Andrews

**Experience glamour, tension, heartbreak and emotion
at 200 HARLEY STREET
in this new eight-book continuity
from Mills & Boon® Medical Romance™**

**These books are also available in eBook format
and in two 200 HARLEY STREET collection bundles
from www.millsandboon.co.uk**

CHAPTER ONE

'MAKE SURE TO get my best side, won't you now?' Declan Underwood joked to the army of paparazzi camped on the front steps of Princess Catherine's Hospital as he parked his motorbike and removed his helmet.

He smiled towards his clicking, whirring audience, who clearly had nothing better to do than chase ambulances on a sunny summer morning, and tried to hide his growing irritation. The last thing he needed was more unwarranted delays, today of all days. He was not in the mood to be polite.

Making his way up the pale stone steps, he batted away questions like a tennis ace.

'Is Princess Safia here?' someone shouted from behind a long lens. 'Is she going to make a full recovery? Will she be scarred for life?'

'Now, come on, give a guy a break. I can't hear one for the other.' Toeing both the clinic's and his own staunch professional line, Declan exhaled slowly and waited for them to settle. 'As you know, ladies and gents, my hands are tied. There's a young girl's privacy to think of. I just can't make any comment.'

Note: make sure the blinds are closed at all times. Move her to a higher floor. Increase security.

Sure, both the Hunter Clinic and the hospital affectionately known as Kate's relied on positive press to further their reach and their work, but this was way too much interest in a young girl fighting for her life, regardless of her background.

Small wonder the Sheikh's staff had been definitive in their demands to uphold their privacy. If any of Declan's family had been involved in a tragedy such as this he'd want to protect them too.

He shuddered and damped down the tight squeeze in his chest. *Had* protected them, for all the good that had done.

'Come on, Declan, it's no coincidence that you—the country's foremost burns reconstruction surgeon—are here and there's a private flight scheduled to arrive from Aljahar any minute.'

Was that Fi…something—the journalist he'd spent a few dates with not so long ago? Trying to use her inside contacts to get more information? Tut-tut. Declan flashed her a particular smile. Similar to the one he'd given her as he'd left for the last time, whenever it was, that said, *Hey, don't push it.*

With all the smiling his jaw muscles had begun to ache, but he knew that the Hunter Clinic boss, Leo, wouldn't want his second-in-command to jeopardise the clinic's new positive relationship with the media. 'I'm so sorry, but you all know that I'm in no position to confirm or deny any rumours. You all know too that even if I did have any idea as to the whereabouts or condition of Princess Safia I couldn't tell you a thing. The Sheikh, quite rightly, is very keen on confidentiality. But I'm sure he and his family appreciate all the concern and will issue a statement as and when appropriate. Now we need to leave the family alone to recover. And I need to go to work. Thank you so much.'

Closing the door behind him to a barrage of

more camera flashes, he exhaled deeply and headed towards the burns unit. Two extensive surgeries, an afternoon clinic and an evening meeting amidst a swirl of media frenzy about a royal with devastating facial burns loomed ahead of him.

It was going to be a very long day.

'You. Yes, you. Stop. Wait.'

A heavily accented raised male voice out in the hospital corridor drew Declan's attention from the notes he was reviewing at his desk over his hastily snatched lunch break.

'What's all that noise on the street? The photographers? Newspapers? His Highness specifically said he wanted Sheikha Safia's arrival to be discreet. His daughter is suffering and she needs peace and quiet. She is devastated about her injuries...'

'Yes, I understand entirely,' an unfamiliar voice with an Antipodean twang replied. 'I have already spoken to Security and they are planning to transfer the Princess through the back door.' Despite the clipped tones the voice was remarkably calm, smoky. Distinctly feminine. Declan put down the papers and listened.

The male voice cut in. 'We understood Mr Underwood himself was going to oversee every detail.'

'Of the surgery and treatment phases, yes, absolutely, but not everything on this list…'

She paused. Declan heard a rustling of paper.

'He's not responsible for the sheet thread count, or the menus or the quality of the glassware… I'll get the services manager to check through all of that…'

'And lilies—we asked for white lilies to decorate her room.'

'Of course. The lilies. Item twenty-two.'

Not an ounce of agitation.

'Unfortunately we don't allow fresh flowers onto the burns unit. It's an infection control issue.'

'No?'

Agitation rippled off the man's voice in streams enough for both of them.

'But for the Sheikha you can do such a thing. She never stays anywhere without lilies. Be warned: His Highness expects high standards and he will get them. His daughter is the very most precious thing to him and he hates her to be upset. I insist you bend the rules.'

'And I insist you leave the medical professionals to *implement* the rules, sir. We have them for a reason. No fresh flowers. The pollen can infect the wounds and make our patients very sick. It's something we're very strict about. No exceptions.'

Declan's interest was piqued. Management had certainly stepped up their game by employing her. He smiled, imagining a stare-off between the mystery woman and the Sheikh's aide.

'Is there anything else? *Sir?*'

'Do not take that tone. The Sheikh is very powerful and can have you removed from your position with just one word.'

The smile was wiped from Declan's face. No one spoke to a member of staff in that way—whoever she was, and however spirited.

He scraped back his chair and walked into the corridor, watching the exchange from a distance, ready to pounce and squash the man if anything got out of hand. He got the feeling the woman wouldn't thank him for interfering and for what that might imply: that she couldn't handle it. When she clearly could. Bringing up his younger sisters had taught him to leave them alone with their arguments and only get involved if things got physical.

'Well, I have a few words I could use too… but I won't.' With a voice so prickly, he hadn't expected the woman to be so young and soft. She had her back to him, but something about her rang bells in Declan's brain. Familiar bells. Warning bells.

The ponytail of light blonde curls, the neat curves in an ice-pink silk blouse and a straight black skirt that skimmed her knees—just. Sky-high black shoes with a razor-sharp heel that surely no one could feasibly walk in but which made her legs look impossibly long and…deeply sexy. A back as straight as a blade, and that voice…smoky…yes…Australian…?

'Let me assure you, sir,' she continued, 'that Safia will receive the finest care in the world here. And if, instead of dealing with your… housekeeping requests, I could finish my preparations for her admission and initial medical assessment, and then actually deal with the injuries she has sustained, we could all make Safia's stay a lot more comfortable.'

The aide stared at her as she rallied.

'I'm sure His Highness would not like to hear that the medical team were held up due to lilies? Glassware? I thought not. We are done here?'

Oh, God. The headache that had bloomed after Declan's sister's early morning phone call threatened to return. This woman was on his medical team? Since when? And why had no one consulted him about it? Declan didn't like surprises. He always liked to know exactly what he was dealing with, and he'd made that damned clear to the powers-that-be.

The Sheikh's aide blanched and bowed slightly. 'Of course. I'm sorry. Of course, Doctor… You know what's best.'

'Yes. Thank you. We do.'

As she turned to watch the aide scuttle away her eyes locked on to Declan's. Her smile slipped completely, and a tinge of pink hit her cheeks. 'Oh.'

The first time she'd shown any hint of bother. But then, within a nanosecond, she'd regained her composure.

'Kiss me.'

A rush of heat and a swirl of memory shook through him. A gold-coloured ballgown that had complemented the colour of the soft curls falling down her back, those startling green eyes commanding his attention, that infuriatingly cocky mouth drawing him in to the most sensual kiss of his life. Only she'd had a sheen of sadness about her too when he'd met her at the bar, knocking back shots. He'd turned it into a game, just to make her smile, which had then turned into something infinitely more interesting.

When was that? Six months ago? The hospital ball? A kiss he'd never found an equal to since, and a woman he'd caught tantalising glimpses of around the surgical unit, at Drake's Bar, and once, possibly, he thought he might have caught a brief whiff of her perfume at the Hunter Clinic. The woman he'd never quite caught up with.

Or even tried to.

And definitely hadn't wanted to.

Because—well…because talking to her, laughing with her, kissing her, had made him want something more. And Declan Underwood never did *more*.

'Good afternoon, Mr Underwood. Adding spying to your list of legendary talents?'

'You are standing right outside my office. It's hardly a covert operation.' Had he ever even known her name? 'Why are you frightening the life out of my esteemed visitors and masquerading as a member of my team? And where the hell is Karen?'

Karen. The timid but efficient junior surgeon who didn't have a bewitching mouth and a dangerous sparkle in her eye.

The woman's mouth twitched. 'White lilies, indeed. If they're all like him we're going to have our work cut out. By all accounts Safia's a little diva. Didn't you hear? Karen's been called away to a family emergency and I've been shifted over to assist until she gets back.'

'Whoa! Slow down. To assist *me*?'

She smiled, but it didn't look as if she was very pleased about the scenario either. He wondered if she was thinking about that kiss too, and how she'd suddenly lost her cool, or her nerve or both, and left him standing on the dance floor trying to work out which tornado had just hit.

Just the thought of it set off a burst of inconvenient heat swimming through his veins.

'Yes, the luck fairies have sprinkled dust on us both today. I'm on your team until Karen gets things sorted.'

Judging by his all too regular experiences of family emergencies she could be away for weeks. His stomach hit his boots. Regardless of what his body might want, mixing work with pleasure was something he avoided at all costs. So he'd be sticking to strictly business.

'And which genius came up with this idea?'

'Ethan Hunter. He called me this morning, said he'd had a call from Karen and was going to run the idea by you, but you were unavailable. He left you a message, apparently. So did she.'

No doubt while Declan's oldest sister had been bending his ear about his middle sister's new boyfriend, the youngest's less than satisfactory university grades and his mother's upcoming birthday plans. He was definitely going to have to set more limits around his personal private time. Sure, hadn't he been trying to do that for the past seventeen years?

'So I miss a call and now I don't get a say about who works with me on one of the most high-profile cases we've had in years?'

'What would you prefer?' Her hands hit her tantalising hips. 'It's me or no one. At least I have a good deal of burns experience. There isn't any other option, with Leo and Lizzie on honeymoon and this place being almost in lockdown with the Sheikh's arrival.'

'No?'

'You could do it all by yourself, but somehow I can't think you'd want to do the junior tasks. Admissions paperwork? Organising bloods?' Her voice rose at the end of every sentence, making it sound as if she was asking an endless list of questions.

'Yes, thank you, I have a full understanding of what is needed. And, it's not that I don't want to do them. I just don't have time.' Stepping up to run the Hunter Clinic in Leo's absence meant he needed more junior staff, not less.

Unbelievable. Declan ran a hand across his neck as he realised he'd been backed into an Antipodean corner. Well, hell, she'd better be as good in surgery as she was at kissing, because he couldn't take any chances—not with his reputation and a young girl's future at stake.

Great. His day had just got a whole lot longer.

'So I hope we don't have a problem here?'

'Absolutely not.'

Oh, but they did. At least Kara did. Declan's Irish lilt curled around her clenched stomach and stroked. Softly. Smoothly. Sexi— *No.* She wasn't allowed to think that. The man was her boss. And an amazing kisser. *Boss.* Kisser. *Boss.* He tipped his chin to one side and gave her the slightest hint of recognition. A nod, perhaps, to their last… *connection…?*

She felt the blush start at her toes and spread, fast, to the top of her head. If only she'd explained her quick getaway—the reason dancing with him had been such a dumb move. Her surprisingly hot bodily response to the first man to hold her in so long. No—it had been a direct response to him and his strong arms and smooth, deep accent. And then, as reality hit, her suddenly very cold feet.

He leaned against his office doorjamb, folded his arms and eyed her with ill-disguised caution.

Shame, because she'd really, really enjoyed that kiss. However wrong. However badly timed. However just damned stupid. And he clearly hardly even remembered her. But then the man had a following of women who thought they could change his commitment-phobic ways. That kiss was probably not a stand-out for him. Luckily she'd put it far behind her.

She summoned every bit of confidence—or at least the show of confidence she'd learned to wear whenever she was in a difficult situation. Eyes forward, shoulders back. Last time she'd felt the need to summon strength she'd been staring down into a casket. The memory rolled off her in waves.

'It's Kara.'

Just in case he'd forgotten her name. Had she even told him it? She remembered looking up. The sight of him standing there in a tuxedo, his hair a messy nonchalant scruff, had stripped the breath from her lungs. She remembered too the way he'd smelled of something spicy and promising as he'd leaned in, the hot shock of an unexpected desire that had matched hers in his deep brown eyes. The earth tilting slightly as he'd spun her in his arms.

'Kara Stephens?'

'Are you asking me? Because if *you* don't know then we really do have a problem.'

Idiot. She decided to speak slowly just so he could understand. Poor puppy. 'My. Name. Is. Kara. Stephens. Only you don't look very happy about something. And I can only assume it's me.'

Seeing as he was staring right at her. All six-foot-too-much, with his arrogant stance and toned body. Even in scrubs she could see the outline of the sculpted abs she'd pressed against, the biceps she'd held as he'd slow-danced with her. The shoulders she'd wound her arms around as his mouth had covered hers.

Heat skittered through her abdomen like a lit fuse wire.

Boss.

Oh. Yes. The first kiss she'd had in too long and it had been off-limits in so many ways. Alcohol, guilt and lust were a heady combination she'd done her best to avoid ever since. Along with him—Mr Break-Your-Heart Underwood.

And now he would refuse to allow her to join the team. Not just for her handling of a tense situation but because of that damned kiss.

'There's a lot at stake here.' He exhaled sharply. 'What do we know about you? Where did you train? What burns experience do you have?'

'Med School in Melbourne, then Perth, then a stint at the Croftwood Institute, Sydney.'

'The Croftwood? Impressive.'

'Yes. And I aced every exam.' Even so, just thinking about her last few days there was like a swift punch to her heart.

But she wouldn't look back. London had been a fresh start, and getting onto this rotation had been an absolute dream job—and then the chance to work alongside a world-class reconstructive surgeon. Until one out-of-character misdemeanour came back to bite her.

Well, kissing the boss certainly wouldn't be happening again. Kissing *anyone* wouldn't be happening. Ever.

'So, what *is* this? A corridor interview? I've helped out at the Hunter Clinic before now. If you want a copy of my CV or references just ask.' Irritation tripped up her spine. 'And, besides, Ethan's already arranged everything.'

Declan's eyebrows rose. 'Without consulting me first. Has he ever actually spoken to you? Seen you in full throttle? Because I listened to a lot of that conversation just now, and the way you—'

She jumped in to defend herself. 'Look, I don't believe in taking risks with clients just because someone who has a lot of money or power asks me to. There's not just Safia to think about, but the other patients on the unit too. Money can buy a lot of things, but it won't buy my professional standards.' She studied his face for a reaction but he wore a mask of impartiality. 'Of course I hope I employed more diplomacy than that.'

He nodded and looked at her. Really looked at her, as if trying to work out a puzzle. 'To be honest, I thought you handled him very well—and you stuck to your guns. It's easy to be swayed by people like that and it's rarely for the good.'

Wow, praise from him now? That was surprising. He had a reputation for being a smooth lover and a competent and exacting doctor, leaving

his patients satisfied and women always wanting more. Which he steadfastly refused to give.

'If you can handle a skin graft as confidently
as you did that aide, then you'll go far.'

The laugh slipped easily from her throat. 'You
know, really I just wanted to tell him where to
get off.'

'Yes. Me too.' He winked, visibly relaxing. 'But
A—you didn't. And *B*—you reassured him of
your competence and professionalism by not cav-
ing in to his demands.'

'I tried my best.'

'Good. I imagine you've more than earned his
respect. You need to gain that too when dealing
with the Sheikh and the press, which is a nec-
essary role with such a high-profile case. We're
a small team with a big responsibility. Are you
up to it?'

'Yes. Absolutely.'

'I would suggest you soften a little for the
Sheikha, though. Diva or not, she's had a very
rough time, she's used to having things her way,
and this accident will have knocked her sideways.' Something passed behind those choco-
late-coloured eyes and his sharp edges melted

away a little. 'Her life has changed forever. She's going to be frightened and in pain and will need a lot of help and reassurance. Not just today but ongoing. Gently.' He eyed her suspiciously. 'You *can* do gently?'

'Of course. Of course.' Hell, she could do roll over and beg if it meant she got to work with someone so talented. Relief flooded through her and she tried to show him her best gentle smile. 'So I'm in, then?'

'For now. It seems I have no choice—and we have to attend to Safia. I'll review your place in my team later.'

'I come highly recommended. Phone the Croftwood and check. I can assure you, you won't be disappointed.'

'No…I doubt that very much.' Declan laughed. 'But, heck, you're a straight talker.'

The same words he'd used at the ball too, when she'd outright demanded he kiss her, right there on the dance floor, when she hadn't been able to stop thinking about how those lips would feel against hers. When she'd wanted something… *him*…to exorcise the past.

She snapped her eyes closed, hoping to goodness he didn't remember that. When she opened them again he was looking at her strangely. Strangely *interested*. The ghost of that kiss hovered between them as his eyes fixed on hers. Yes, he remembered. And if the brief flash of heat was anything to go by he remembered how good it had felt too. That warm glow in her abdomen returned.

She doused it with a quick shot of reality as she began to walk along the corridor towards the burns unit High Dependency ward. The last time she'd got carried away by hearts and flowers and physical desires she'd ended up married. Then endured a swift lesson in a run of all the emotions from *A* to *Z*.

She'd packed a lifetime of hurt into those few years and she had no intention of making the same mistakes again. So much had sent her reeling, trying to work out how something that had started out so pure had ended so damned soiled. Focusing on her career was a lot less painful— but then, that was what had caused all the trouble in the first place.

'It comes from my upbringing, I guess.'

'Oh? What?' He fell into step beside her.

'Forthrightness. I'm an army brat. Always moving around. If you don't say what you think straightaway you'll be packed up and on the move before you get another chance.' There'd been a lot of lost chances before she'd learnt that lesson. 'Although it can get me into trouble.'

'I imagine it can.'

It already has, his look said. On that dance floor.

His dark pupils flared. 'Australian army?'

'Yes. My parents met as new recruits and both followed military careers.'

'Exciting? Interesting?'

'Difficult…for them both, I think. One member of a family in the military is hard enough, but both parents trying to work up the career ladder meant a lot of discussing, juggling, arguing, vying for priority. What their child wanted came at the bottom of the pecking order.'

She'd learnt to speak loudly and fight hard to get heard.

'Constantly moving and growing up on bases makes you grow a thick skin and a quick mouth.

But, hey, I can shoot in a straight line and hit a target at a hundred metres.'

'Me too.' At her frown he illuminated, 'Farm boy.'

Now, *that* was a surprise. He oozed class and rubbed easy broad shoulders with a rich and famous clientele. 'Irish farm boy to Harley Street surgeon? That must be an interesting story.'

'Not really.' His smile disappeared and he looked at her as if she'd stepped over some imaginary line. Shoving his hands in his pockets, he quickened his step. She got the message—working together was okay, even kissing wasn't a step too close, but sharing intimate details…? Never. And that suited her just fine. The less she shared about the life she'd left the better too.

As they entered the unit Kara observed an atmosphere of calm chaos—a feeling that matched her stomach. Although being surrounded by busy people was much less intense than being alone with Declan. She knew how to act here. There were protocols and policies, standards and codes. Out there in the real world, the dating world, the rules were far too confusing.

She breathed out and put her professional hat

firmly on. 'So, all the staff are up to speed with privacy requests, and everyone has been told not to comment at all to anyone phoning in, regardless of who they say they are.'

'Excellent.' He nodded, walking into the room he'd personally had allocated to Safia. 'This looks perfect, but keep the bed away from the window.' He peered through the blinds down to the road outside. 'No one should be able to see her here on this floor. As soon as she arrives we'll need to check her pain levels and medication. I don't want her to be scared we're going to hurt her when we remove the dressings. Then I'll need an immediate blood screen to make sure she's haemodynamically stable. Then…then we can take a good look and see what we're dealing with.'

'No worries.' She picked up the clipboard on the end of the bed and checked all the correct paperwork was in place.

'So.' Declan glanced around. 'What's her ETA?'

Kara glanced at her watch. 'Ten minutes.'

'Excellent.'

Although this was a devastating case, he looked

wired and ready. This was another side of him she'd heard about but hadn't yet encountered: his infectious enthusiasm for his work. It seemed the man had many sides apart from his infamous charm, and yet—as she'd witnessed—a mysterious unwillingness to open up about anything personal.

Which was fine. Because she would not let that kiss get in the way of her job. Or let that body of his distract her from her purpose. Or those eyes… Her stomach did a little cartwheel… Those eyes staring at her with playful teasing.

'So, Kara Stephens, it looks like we have just enough time to check out the sheets.'

'What?' Her pulse rocketed.

The smile he flashed her was nothing less than wicked. 'Thread count?'

'Oh. Yes. Of course.' And she blushed again, because one mention of sheets and their thread count was the furthest thing from her mind.

CHAPTER TWO

'I SAID, DON'T touch me.' A pair of dark, frightened eyes, trying desperately hard to be brave, peered out through a face covered in bandages. 'Go away.'

Kara leaned in to the bed and lowered her voice. This was getting precisely nowhere, but she could not and would not rush her patient. 'I'm sorry, Safia, but we are going to have to remove the dressings sometime so we can see your burns and then treat them. We just want to help.'

'What part of *go away* don't you understand?' Her muffled voice was thick with the tears the teenager steadfastly refused to allow. 'Leave me alone.'

'Does it hurt? I can give you some more medicine to take the pain away. You must tell me if you need more.'

The girl shook her head.

'I'll do it slowly and carefully. I promise.'

But Safia raised a heavily bandaged arm and pulled the sheet over her head. The spaghetti of tubes reverberated at the swift move. An alarm rang out.

Kara took a moment to compose herself, checked the drips were patent, reset the machines and tried again. And she would continue trying until the poor girl agreed. However long it took. The theatre was booked from eight tomorrow morning. That gave her about eighteen hours. She hoped it would be enough. 'Your Highness...'

'Let me try.' Sheikh El-Zayad of Aljahar, the girl's father, stepped forward. 'For goodness' sake, Safia, do as you're told. We've been waiting for twenty-five minutes for your bandages to come off and it's getting past a joke. The doctors can't do their job and you won't get better.'

'I'm never going to get better. This is it. Scarred for life. So get used to it.'

The Sheikh frowned. 'Do as the doctor says. Stop behaving like a child.'

She is a child. Kara bit that thought back. He had just endured the worst thing any parent could live through—watching his child suffer—and no doubt wanted her full co-operation to get better.

But seventeen was barely mature, and the ramifications of such injuries would surely make anyone scared and fractious.

She shot a look over to Declan as he finished his conversation with the Sheikh's wife, psychologically prepping her for the forthcoming procedures and long-term treatment plan. Throughout the long thirty minutes of cajoling and waiting she'd felt Declan's eyes on her, assessing, weighing her up, his playful teasing forgotten, cemented now into something much more serious.

'So to recap—' He leaned forward to speak to Safia's parents. 'We're planning to do a series of operations over the next few weeks. Because Safia's wounds are of differing severity and depth each one will be in its own individual recovery phase. Some wounds, I understand from her notes, are ready for closure or grafting tomorrow. Some will have to wait for closure because they need debriding. I'll keep you fully informed as we proceed.'

Declan's demeanour was one of total calm and efficiency, yet he commanded an authority that stood him apart as he spoke.

'Now, it's getting a bit hot in here. Perhaps

Your Highnesses might like a tour of the facility? There's a particularly nice view out over the river from the roof garden. It's very private up there and shouldn't be busy. In fact, I can make sure it isn't. And I can organise some tea for you both.'

Safia's mother nodded and wafted in front of her face with her hand. 'Oh, please. Yes. I need some fresh air.' Leaning in to her daughter, she whispered, 'That is, of course, if you don't mind, darling Safia? We won't stay away for long.'

The sheets moved a little. 'Go. All of you. Leave me here. Forever.'

A quick phone call later and Safia, Kara and Declan were alone.

But now what? Even without her parents in the room it was going to be tough convincing Safia to comply.

Kara was just about to broach the dressings conversation again when Declan laughed. 'Well, would you look at that *eejit*.'

'What? Where?' Kara frowned as she looked over to him. His focus was on a pile of magazines on the table. The latest teen heart-throb was emblazoned on the front cover of *BFF!* magazine, which had been covered in pink glitter hand-drawn hearts. 'Oh, that's Liam from Oblivion.'

'I don't care where he's from,' he continued. 'He looks like he needs a decent feed and a new belt. Are those his grandaddy's trousers he's wearing? Because they don't seem to fit.'

Kara looked up again and noticed he was watching the sheet move down. Just a little.

She joined in. 'How can you say that? Don't break my heart. Liam is hot, hot, *hot*. And what do you know, Mr Fuddy-Duddy? Those baggy trousers are all the rage. Maybe you should get a pair.'

'Maybe I should. D'you think all the girls would come screaming after me then?' He gave a very poor rendition of Oblivion's number one hit. '"That's what makes me looooove you…"'

'Screaming to get away from you, more like. Save our poor ears and stick to the day job.' She leaned closer to the sheet that was now making little noises that sounded a lot like hesitant sur-prised laughter. 'Great doctor, really, don't let the singing put you off. I heard that Oblivion's doing a tour soon—they're playing in London in a few weeks.' And going to see her favourite singer might well give Safia the motivation she needed to get better.

The girl sighed. 'He played at my sixteenth birthday party. He said I was beautiful.' Safia slowly pulled the sheet back. 'But he wouldn't say that now.'

Declan sat next to the bed and looked at her. Kara wondered what on earth he could say to make her feel better. 'Don't you know you've gorgeous eyes, Safia? Beautiful. A boy could lose himself in there.'

'Once, maybe. But not now.'

'Oh, definitely now.'

Safia met Declan's gaze, still cautious, but she didn't tell them to leave.

Seizing this moment of calm, Declan reached out and began to remove a dressing with painstaking care. When Safia put her hand out to stop him he gave her a quick shake of his head and a reassuring smile. The girl lay back and closed her eyes.

Kara opened another dressing pack and covered the bed as he kept his focus on his patient and smiled softly and gently, as if she was the most beautiful person in the world, the only person in the world. As if the horrendous discolouration and raw melted skin didn't make his heart jerk or his professional eye wonder how in hell they could ever restore her back to her previous beauty.

She'd heard about his slick surgical skills and knew how well respected he was. Heck, the Sheikh had personally requested Declan did the surgery—and judging by his extensive client list both here and at the Hunter Clinic he was well sought after. So she hadn't expected a doctor as talented as Declan to have such grounded humanity.

'There. There. Nearly done now. You're doing grand, sweetheart. Just grand. It's not nearly so bad as I thought it'd be.'

He spoke in a mesmerising, soothing voice that felt as if he was stroking the raw wounds back together again. Kara didn't think she'd ever seen anything so touching.

'I bet you've broken a few hearts already, Safia?'

The girl opened her eyes and gave him a sad smile. 'Yes…you mustn't tell my father.'

'Cross my heart.'

'But I never will again. Who's going to love me with a face like this? Skin like this?' She lifted the arms she'd tried to shield her face with and showed him the skin that had been so damaged. Finally tears began to fall. 'Don't tell me that beauty's skin-deep. Or that scars are sexy. Because they're not. And please don't tell me that looks don't matter—because in my world they do.'

And that was the heart of the matter. A young girl's life was broken and no one could truly fix it.

Kara's throat closed tight.

Declan ran his hand over the girl's hair. 'Ah, now, sweetheart. That's it. That's it. I know. Believe me, I know. Let it out. Just let it go.'

'I'm…so…tired…of being brave,' Safia sobbed. 'Of trying to pretend it's okay when it's not. And all they do is make promises that I'll be back to normal soon. How can I?' She looked up at him, eyes pleading but with a glimpse of trust. 'Can you make me better, Dr Underwood?'

'Call me Declan, please. Actually, call me Dec if you like—my sisters call me that.'

'Okay.' Safia nodded and smiled again. 'Dec.'

'Listen, Safia, I will be honest with you because you deserve that at the very least. I can't ever make it go away completely.' His voice caught a little as he thumbed away the girl's tears.

A few months ago Kara had watched him smooth his way across a dance floor, his charm and flirtatious manner catching her in a moment of weakness. But there was a genuine depth to him that she hadn't imagined.

He cleared his throat. 'But I promise I can make it a whole lot better. Will you let me try?'

'At first glance, Safia's burns are a mix of partial and full thickness—some will need further debridement and then grafting,' Declan said to Kara as they grabbed a coffee en route to the media room.

His head was a whirl of the emotions that always shook through him at this stage of assessment—emotions he had a tight hold of and would never allow to interfere with any professional judgement. Flashbacks from seventeen years ago haunted him each time he removed a dressing, but they made him more determined to improve his skills and techniques.

Another woman damaged. It made him sick to his stomach.

His new junior surgeon took a sip of coffee, oblivious to what was going on in his head. Which was a damned fine thing—no one needed to know his motivations, just his achievements. She smiled and his gut tightened. He put it down to stress.

'So, Declan, do you prefer autograft or zenograft?'

'It depends entirely on the situation. We can get a better look at the viability of the skin and the underlying bed tomorrow in Theatre and take it from there.'

Eyebrows peaked. 'We?'

'Yes. Okay, you can scrub in tomorrow. You did well in there. Teenagers are often the most difficult cases to deal with. They don't know how to act—they're kids at heart but trying desperately to be adult. We have to get the next few days right. How we deal with these burns will have a huge effect on the rest of that girl's life. Both physically and psychologically.' From his experience the mental scarring was often the worst and could change the very core of an injured person for life.

Kara nodded, eyes alight, blonde curls shivering. Something unbidden shivered through him too. She'd been damned good at handling Safia, so he was pleased to have her on his team. But… really it was more than that. She was a weird kind of unsettling—and yet settling at the same time.

Her eyes narrowed. 'I can't believe the admitting hospital staff didn't think of offering her some anxiolytics to help raise her mood. Maybe we could have a chat with her about that too?'

'I guess they were dealing with her immediate issues, like keeping her alive.' He held the door open to let her through. Which was an action he immediately regretted. The barrage of flashing bulbs that had greeted him that morning met them as they stepped into the room, catching her unawares—but he was interested to see just how well she could handle this part of the job.

'Is Princess Safia here now?'

'What can you tell us about her condition?'

Next to him Kara stood tall, her shoulders snapped back, confident. Declan held back a smile as he watched her survey the room with a tilt of her chin. She wore her army upbringing in her stance, and he had no doubt she would answer the press's queries with aplomb and professionalism, but he wasn't game enough to test her with that just yet. In fact he wasn't game enough to do anything that involved any more contact with her than he had to. The woman was mysteriously alluring. So that meant avoiding her at all costs.

No doubt a better man would probably not even allow her to assist him when his hormones were acting as if he was eighteen years old again. But he had stopped being a better man a long time ago—the day he'd lost all faith in love.

Kara's scent wove around him…something exotic that reminded him of brilliant blue skies and endless heat and the tang of flowers on the breeze. His abdomen tightened as seemingly endless heat rippled through him too.

He took a step away and glanced at the floor, trying to take a moment to focus. But all he could see were those ridiculous but sexy shoes, slender tanned ankles leading up to the hem of her skirt, and farther on up to a place where his imagination ran wild.

He ran a hand through his hair and shook that

image from his head. *Damn fool.* Since when had he allowed a woman to distract him at work? Since the second he'd seen her firing back at the Sheikh's aide? Or was it that kiss?

He quieted the audience with a raise of his hands and a smile. Keep them on side and they might actually let him have time free to do his job. 'Thanks for coming to this meeting. We didn't want you getting chilly out there. We're already busy enough without dealing with hypothermic journalists as well. Hope you enjoyed the tea and biscuits.'

Laughter rippled round the room. He waited for it to stop.

'Thank you for your patience, everyone. I have permission from Safia's family to confirm that she is indeed now here at Princess Catherine's Hospital and that I am treating her as an inpatient. I'm sure you are all aware of the car accident she had a few days ago. I can confirm also that, thanks to the great care she received at Aljahar Hospital, she is now in a stable condition, but her injuries mean that she will be under my care for some time. The family again asks for privacy. Thank you.'

'What does the Sheikh think about this?'

'Naturally His Highness is devastated about his daughter's injuries, but he is working with us to get the best possible outcome. Of course we are deeply honoured to have him here.'

'How long will Safia be with you?'

'That depends entirely on her progress and response to treatment. It could be a few weeks.' He paused for effect. 'Okay, I don't think there is anything more we can tell you. Either myself or a member of my team...' He indicated to Kara and she stepped forward and smiled, self-confidence rippling off her. 'This is Ms Stephens, who will be working with me. Either one of us will be updating you on Safia's progress as and when appropriate.'

'They don't teach you that at medical school.' Kara joked as they walked towards the afternoon out-patient clinic. 'They should have "Dealing with the Press" lessons. Confidentiality is such a thorny issue—especially when you're treating someone famous.'

'No one wants to know about you if you're not. But this is a high-profile issue and we have to deal with it—it's just another part of the job. You have to be careful not to give away too much information but just enough to keep the hacks satisfied.'

'It's a bit of a tightrope. I can see I'll have to be careful.'

'I can fix you up with our in-house Head of PR, Lexi, at the Hunter Clinic if you like? She could give you some pointers if you think you might need them.' Why, oh, why was he even thinking of getting further involved in this woman's life? 'But I reckon you'll be fine.'

'Really?' Her smile was genuine. 'Thanks. I'll see how I go.'

That compliment sat between them as they neared the clinic. He'd have to be careful about that—giving her the wrong impression. But something about Kara drew him to her. Even with his internal alarm bells blaring.

As he tried to walk down the narrow corridor without brushing against her and risking an escalation of his already over-excited libido she spoke. 'So, how many sisters do you have?'

'What?' He stopped short, still getting used to her forthrightness. Maybe it was an Aussie thing. No, maybe it was just a Kara thing. 'Sorry?'

'You were telling Safia about your sisters. *"They call me Dec,"* you said, or something.'

'Why do you need to know?'

Her forehead furrowed into a deep V and her eyes sparked with humour and intrigue. 'I don't *need* anything. I was just making conversation. It's what human beings do to fill that very long gap between birth and death. Communication.'

She held his gaze and it felt as if she was throwing down a gauntlet. One he could run with or one he could walk away from.

'Only, I don't have any siblings, and I always thought it'd be nice to have some. It's just a chat, Declan, as we while away the minutes. Not an interrogation.'

She was right. It was just talking. It wasn't exactly baring his soul. And he'd always been a sucker for gauntlets. 'Well, if I were you I'd rejoice in your single-child-dom, Kara—because, trust me, you do *not* need four sisters.'

'Four? Wow.'

'All younger. All a giant pain in the ass...'

She laughed. 'Growing up amongst that must have been busy. But fun, though?'

'It was messy...crazy...loud. Very loud. And

awash with wayward hormones.' Remembering the madcap phone call that morning, he shrugged, smiling to himself. They might well be irritating, but they were his. 'Still is.'

'But it explains how you can deal so well with kids like Safia.'

'I don't know about *well*. The way I see it, all girls want to be treated like princesses. It just so happens she *is* one. But underneath they're generally the same. They worry about how they look, who they're becoming, what they want to do with their lives. Love. Boys…yeah, boys mostly, if my lot were anything to go by. Trouble all round.'

He'd had the job of being the man of the house thrust upon him way too young and had had to make sure they somehow had the basics, like enough food to eat, even when they hadn't had the money to buy it. Then as they grew up he'd watched his sisters have their hearts broken and wanted to kill the culprits, but decided not to. He had negotiated conversations about teenage pregnancy and underage sex, about dating rules and bedtimes, had nursed sisters with period pains and migraines and tummy aches of dubious origin. And finally he'd escaped only when he'd known they were all grown up and relatively safe. *Escaped* being a geographical rather than a psychological term.

And yet with all his experience he still couldn't fathom the workings of a woman's brain. Except that he definitely knew when it was time to leave—which was around about the time she started talking about a future.

Kara laughed. 'But I can see the pride in your eyes and hear it in your voice. You love them all, clearly.'

'Yes, I probably do—but don't ever let them know that or they'll take even more advantage. And I chose a job hundreds of miles away from them just to put a good stretch of Irish Sea between us.' He laughed along with her. 'Thankfully none of them are any good at swimming, most of them get seasick, and they can't afford the airfare—otherwise I'm damned sure they'd be here. Making my life hell in England too.'

But in reality he might as well be living back home, seeing as they couldn't or wouldn't make a single damned decision without him. Which was why he kept his tiny slice of private time simple. No getting involved on any kind of scale. His life was already too full of responsibilities and women without taking on another one.

Kara smirked as they entered the out-patients' reception. 'I guess you have to go where the work is.'

'Is that what you did? It's a long way from Sydney to London, and you didn't have four sisters dragging at your heels.'

'I needed a change. Coming here was a good move for lots of reasons.'

The way she said that didn't convince him that her move to London had been a positive choice. She rubbed her thumb around the base of her left-hand ring finger as her eyes darted upwards. She seemed to be searching for an answer. Not the truth, just an answer.

Seemed everyone had their demons. And he was inexplicably intrigued, even though he'd made it his life's purpose never to be drawn into a woman's dramas unless he had a failsafe get-out plan.

She peered up at him and his world tilted a little. He wasn't used to scrutiny, or to someone pushing him for more—or wanting to give it. So why would she have this effect on him?

'And you, Declan? Why choose burns reconstruction when you could have the glory and
financial reward of cosmetic surgery? Breast
augmentation? Tattoo removal? Enhancement of
the rich and famous? Why specialise in burns?'

The way she adeptly deflected the conversation told him she didn't want to delve deeper
into her reasons for coming here and he could
respect that.

But, hell… His chest tightened by degrees. The
questions she was asking. Questions people asked
him periodically, but not usually straight after a
conversation about his family. Or after a consul-
tation with a badly scarred woman. Questions
that he didn't want to answer. Wouldn't answer.
Wouldn't no matter how much her sharp green
eyes reached down into his soul and tugged.

'Ah, you know…it's just how it worked out.'

And with that he turned and walked away.

CHAPTER THREE

SO THE GREAT Declan Underwood had walls so high even a simple conversation couldn't penetrate them, Kara mused as she scrubbed up the next morning. She would do well to remember that.

She should have remembered it last night too as she lay in the dark and thought about the way she'd fitted so neatly into his arms on the ballroom floor all those months ago. And the way he'd tasted—of something fresh and new, of an experienced man. Not like the previous kisses she'd experienced from the kid she'd known her whole life. The way Declan's big broad shoulders—a match for any Aussie rugby league player's—looked as if they could carry the weight of a million problems. But she hadn't wanted to share hers. No, she'd had other things on her mind. Nice other things. Naughty other things.

And she should have remembered it too when

Declan's face had been the last thing she'd thought of before she'd fallen asleep. Almost the first thing to flash through her brain as her alarm clock blared. The very first thing, as always, had been the thick thud of loss. The reality of how much her life had changed. The tiny slash of almost white skin where her wedding ring used to be.

But this morning the sharp sting of regret hadn't been quite so harsh.

Even so, she still hadn't thought about the barriers Declan had erected, or the way he'd turned his back on her. She'd simply remembered how sweet it had felt when he'd hammered against her barriers with one scorching touch of his mouth.

The same mouth that was now grinning at her as he walked into the scrub room. She put the little heart jig down to excitement at the forthcoming surgery and nothing to do with the sudden scent of soap and spice, or the soft brown eyes, or the way his biceps muscles lengthened as he reached for the tap.

The V neck of his top bared a tantalising amount of suntanned chest and she imagined what might be underneath the navy cotton scrubs… Sometimes a working knowledge of anatomy did a girl nothing but harm. Especially first thing in the morning.

He opened a sterile pack and laid it on a trolley, put on the surgical cap and mask and began washing with the nailbrush, rubbing small circles over his fingers, hands, up his arms.

'Good morning, Ms Stephens. Sleep well?'

'Hi. Um… Yes, thanks.' *Liar.* Sleeping and thoughts of Declan Underwood were not satisfactory bedfellows.

She dried her hands, pulled on her gown and snapped on her gloves. Took a quick check in the mirror and relaxed. There was no way there would be any kind of sexual vibes happening today—hair in a cap and body in oversized scrubs really didn't scream goddess or available. Or any kind of *hot-for-you.* Thank God.

'And shouldn't it be top of the mornin'?'

'A whole millennia of culture reduced to the diddly-diddly. Sure, and we're all leprechauns.' He laughed, his eyes crinkling at the corners.

That tall, broad body was the furthest thing from a leprechaun she could imagine.

'And shouldn't it be g'day?'

'Cobber. If you're going the whole reductive stereotype, it should be g'day, cobber. Or sheila. And don't forget the cork hat.'

'Same language but not a lot of commonality, eh? That's a shame. A real shame.' He dried his hands, gowned up and smiled. 'Perhaps we should try to forge some middle ground, Kara? There's a whole lot more I could teach you about Irish culture... In the interests of international relations. Obviously.'

'Obviously.' Was that a come on? Or just a joke? *Aaargh.* Having been a one-man woman for so long, she didn't understand the language of flirting.

No matter. She didn't have time to compute. At that moment he stepped back, catching her unawares in the tiny airless room. His hip brushed against hers and she turned too quickly, slamming body to body against him. Tingles ran the length of her spine as her heart continued a jig that was *all* diddly-diddly.

'Oh. I'm sorry.'

His gaze met hers and for a split second, maybe two, he watched her. Some weird connection tugged between them. His eyes misted with

something akin to confusion, along with an un-
mistakable heat that seemed to whoosh all the
oxygen from her lungs.

His arms were splayed high in front of him,
so as not to desterilise them, but that made his
face closer to hers. Damn lucky he was wearing
a mask or his mouth would have been in frank
kissing range.

The heat coming off him was electric, almost
palpable. He smiled. Or at least she thought he
did—hard to tell under that mask, but his forehead crinkled and laughter lines creased at his
temples.

'Nothing to apologise for, Kara. No harm done.
In fact...I like it.'

So did she. And, oh, if it wasn't enough just
to have that soft accent tug on her heartstrings.

She swallowed through a dry throat, pushed
the Theatre door open with her hip and gestured
for him to walk through in front of her. How the
hell would she spend a morning in surgery staring at those eyes, listening to that voice, looking
at that body, and get out whole? He was going
to reduce her to a hot mess of unruly hormones.

So she would take a leaf out of his book and

refuse to engage in conversation about anything other than the task at hand.

Forcing words out was harder than she'd expected. 'So. How's Safia doing? When I popped up to see her an hour or so ago she didn't say much. I got the impression she was hanging out for you to visit.'

He shrugged. 'She's okay, I suppose. She's scared about the operation. Actually, she's scared about the pain. I did warn her about the initial sting of the graft sites, but we talked about pain relief and I've discussed it with Paul, the anaesthetist, so she should be well covered when she wakes up. I've warned her we can't fix it all today, and that she'll have negative pressure dressings on and to expect lots of tubes.'

'Great. And the parents? They seemed to think you were going to restore her to her former beauty.'

His left shoulder hiked. 'I had a long and honest meeting with them last night and showed them the digital blueprint we mocked up of how we hope Safia will look after the surgeries. They understand that we can only do so much, and that a lot is dependent on how Safia heals, the kind of scarring we get, whether she complies with physio. Although I still think they're a little unrealistic. My main concern is that she maintains function in those hands. But she's here and agreeing to treatment and that's the best we can hope for right now.'

He turned as the technician wheeled Safia in.

'Okay. Let's go. Hands first and then her face. We'll start with debriding.'

It was like watching an artist at work. A study in concentration, he was efficient but thorough. Instead of the brash rock music favoured by a lot of surgeons she'd worked with Declan chose something that was uplifting but gentle. There was a positivity to it, something that soothed yet entranced.

Or was that just him? Kara couldn't tell.

Even though he was the senior member of staff he treated everyone in the room with the same respect and took his time to explain his procedures.

'See here?' He gestured to Safia's damaged cheek. 'If we want to get a good result we have to consider the whole area as a unit, not just the part that's damaged, otherwise the scarring will be ridged. It's a multi-thickness burn—only second degree here, but here, where her face hit the dashboard, it's deeper. So I'm going to have to use a split thickness graft.'

'And attach it with absorbent stitches? Or glue?' She passed him some gauze just as he reached out for it. The third time she'd anticipated his next move.

'In this case, I'd say stitches.' He shook his head, as if trying to get rid of a wayward thought. 'What did you do in Sydney?'

'Oh, this and that. Music concerts, swimming, going out with friends. My husband was away a lot so I was able…to…study…' She slowed right down and noticed all eyes were on her.

Surgery.

That deep, luscious voice was asking about the Croftwood's choice of surgical closure techniques—not about her private life. Her chest tightened. *Duh.* There went her credibility.

'Er…usually stitches. But glue if we thought the dressing wouldn't be knocked or slip easily. Really it depended on the patient and the damaged area.'

She flatly refused to look him in the eye. Flatly. But she knew she was the single beacon of bright red in an otherwise white and sterile environment.

'Husband?'

The accusation hung in the air along with the ghost of that kiss. As she turned to look at him his eyebrows rose.

God. She focused instead on the tube of antibiotic ointment in a dish to her left. Did he really think she'd have kissed him if she'd had a husband? When she'd entered her marriage it had been with an innocent and pure belief in forever. Too bad forever couldn't happen.

'Not any more.'

'Okay.' Declan's voice was impassive. 'Great work, team. Thanks for your help. She's good to go to recovery. I'll head up to have a chat with Mum and Dad after the next surgery.'

The technicians got busy taking Safia out and preparing for the next patient, leaving Kara alone for snatched minutes with Declan. Goddamn, the man stirred a smorgasbord of emotions in her. Right now it was a huge dose of embarrassment.

'Er... About before...'

'Kara...'

He glanced up from the surgery list he was

reading. *About what?* his look said. *The kiss? The husband?*

He removed his surgical mask, his mouth tipping up halfway to a wry smile. 'Your life is your life. You don't have to explain.'

'I shouldn't have rabbited on.'

'Oh, no, to the contrary, we were all riveted. Concerts? Swimming?'

The omission of *husband* made her faux pas even more mortifying.

She shrugged. 'What can I say? We're a nation of water babies. Sydney's by the ocean.'

'And it gets very hot and there are snakes and spiders and lots of things that could kill you. I know.' His voice had developed a harder tone now. 'It's also a very long way from here and people can get lonely.'

Was that what he thought? That she'd hooked up with him because she was homesick? Because she missed her husband? Because she regretted everything that had happened?

Well, wasn't it? She didn't know any more.

Four days later Declan was sitting at his desk making a poor show of doing the paperwork, checking staffing levels for the Hunter Clinic and keeping track of patients' results.

He exhaled long and hard as the paper stack wobbled. It had been a very long week so far and tomorrow promised no let up. There were more surgeries booked, no doubt a scuffle through the media camped outside and a report due for Leo when he returned from honeymoon.

So why the hell, when he was supposed to be working, was he daydreaming about soft lips and green eyes? About a junior surgeon who anticipated his every move in Theatre, whose scent he could recognise at fifty paces, who seemed to have a direct line to his brain.

And his groin.

And was married. Or had been. Still, she wore no ring, and she'd been adamant that it was over.

He smiled at the thought of her ill-concealed blushes. She had a cool exterior, and could handle herself very well, but there was an unexpected softness about her too. A vulnerability that she hid, or tried to hide.

So he'd stayed out of her way as much as possible, because she was a heady mix of things that seemed to attract him more than they should.

But avoiding contact with her hadn't worked; he couldn't get the damned woman out of his head.

'Hey. Just passing by en route to an emergency surgery. All good here?'

Friend and colleague Ethan Hunter stood in the doorway, his usual reluctant smile playing hooky. Dressed in scrubs, he looked primed for action. And Ethan always took that very seriously.

He'd been offered the position of Hunter Clinic head in his brother's absence but had somehow managed to persuade Declan to take that particular mantle, talking up Declan's silky PR skills. Declan had agreed—it was all good management experience. And, given the trauma Ethan had been through and his fight back to health, Declan hadn't wanted to refuse.

But this was also the guy responsible for Kara invading his thoughts. Declan could either tell him the truth—that she was quietly driving him mad—or get on with it. The very private Ethan wasn't exactly the kind of guy to confide 'deep and meaningful' to.

Declan shuffled some paper. 'All good, I suppose. Trying to get to grips with the accounts for when Leo gets back.'

At the mention of his brother's name Ethan stiffened. 'I'm sure you'll manage fine. Hey, how's Kara fitting in? I've heard good reports.'

Declan shrugged, trying not to give too much away. If he was struggling with anything he wouldn't let anyone know. And surely Ethan knew about their kiss at the ball? It was public knowledge.

'Okay. But I'll be happy when Karen gets back. She knows the routine—how I like things.' And she didn't pre-empt everything he did.

But the way Kara's eyes had swirled with a zillion different emotions—none of them warm and fuzzy ones—when she'd spoken about her husband had drawn him to her even more. Having nursed his sisters through enough broken hearts to add more than a few grey hairs to his head, he knew better than even to ask Kara what her story was...but for some reason he was beyond intrigued.

'Hmm. I did wonder about allocating her to you, but short-staffed is short-staffed...'

So Ethan must know about the kiss. It was Declan's own stupid fault for mixing work with fun.

Ethan frowned. 'It's not like you to not gel with someone...'

Oh, yes. He gelled okay. Too damned much. Gelling wasn't the problem. *Un*-gelling was. 'Ah, well, you know...'

'I presume you've had the setting the guide-lines talk? Taken the "this is how *I* do things" approach?'

'We've been busy. You know what it's like with a media circus on your doorstep.'

'So demarcate some time—take her for a quick coffee, a drink. There's nothing wrong with her medical practice, though?'

'Hell, no. She's an excellent surgeon. But as it's probably only a short rotation with me I don't think we need bother with all that *getting to know you* stuff.'

'No?' Ethan ran a hand over his jaw. He looked tired. And hassled. 'Try to get on with her, Declan. There's been too much bad blood run-ning through this place for too long.' He checked his watch. 'A drink. A coffee. I don't care what you do. Just do it. I want to hear things are going smoothly, right? I could do without the stress of more work-related worries.'

Declan guessed Ethan was referring to the complicated relationship between the Hunter brothers.

'Okay, boss.'

The man must have been a force to be reckoned with in the army. Fighting the urge to salute, Declan slammed the laptop shut and shoved it into his backpack, made his way to the hospital exit and breathed deeply, filling his lungs with disappointingly stuffy city air. What he needed was a good long ride on his bike to clear the cobwebs. A cosy chat be damned. What he needed was a Kara-free life.

Thankfully the car park was devoid of journalists, leaving him a clear path towards his motorbike. He strode ahead, helmet in hand, the evening sunshine glinting off the chrome handlebars.

Out of the corner of his eye he caught a movement. Someone else leaving the hospital, heading quickly—or as quickly as she could in a pair of red satin stilettoes that made his heart stutter—towards the bus stop. Not quick enough, though, as the bus sailed past, leaving her stamping her pretty shoes against the tarmac.

At closer inspection he confirmed it was Kara, her hair loose down her back, which drew his eye to her slim waist, nipped in by a fitted cardigan and then lower, to her perfectly shaped backside encased in skinny black trousers. A shot of heat fizzed through him as if someone had flicked a switch in his body.

So he should have just ridden away. But before he knew what he was doing he'd strolled right on up to her.

Ethan's orders, right? Taking one for the team for the sake of no bad blood. 'Hey. Dr Down-Under.'

'Watch it!' She jumped round to face him, at the same time lunging at his throat in a well-practised self-defence karate chop move, her palm almost connecting to his chin.

In a knee-jerk reaction he took a step back and grabbed her palm. He didn't think for one minute she'd have a qualm about trying to floor him and using her stiletto as a weapon. 'Hey! Over-reaction, much?'

'Oh. It's you. You nearly gave me a heart attack.' She shook her hand free from his grip and frowned.

'Lucky we're outside a hospital, then.' A short, hot kiss of life sprang to the forefront of his mind.

'Do you often jump out at women from dark corners, wearing…'

Her eyes widened as her gaze travelled over his dark grey T-shirt and jeans. A suit and tie were all well and good for an office day, or a riding the underground day, but not for a bike to work day.

Her throat bobbed up and down as she swallowed. 'Wearing…a leather jacket…'

'Only on special occasions.' When she'd stopped staring and had seemed to gather her wits again he grinned. 'You missed the bus.'

'Thank you, Einstein.' A deep V formed along her forehead. 'He must have been blind not to see me. I was waving enough.'

'Blind, indeed. Any man worth his salt would have stopped just for those shoes. But you were quite a distance from the bus stop—maybe trainers might be a better choice for running next time.'

She looked down, raised an ankle and turned it this way and that to look at her shoes. He followed her every movement, mesmerised. She had damned fine legs.

Purely an objective observation. Obviously.

An eyebrow peaked. 'Ah, come on—never, *ever* compromise fashion for practicality. Oh…' Her eyes toured his body again and landed on his jacket. 'You just did.'

But he could tell from the hunger in those startling green pupils that she liked what she saw. 'Steady, now. This jacket saved me from a skin-to-tarmac pebble-dashing after a collision with a drunk driver. It's my favourite.'

'Ouch. Lucky escape.' She ran her hand up the zipper and regarded the scuffed black fabric. 'By "favourite," I suppose you mean old?'

'Some things you should never get rid of. Now…'

A drink, Ethan had ordered. A chat. Guidelines. He could do that.

'I don't suppose you've time for a quick drink? Coffee? I'd like to have an informal meeting… a chat about our patient list, Safia, the surgery, guidelines…' *And the kiss. And the husband.*

Hell, he knew too much about Kara Stephens, and *so* not enough. And his drama-free night fizzed into nothing under the cynical watchful eye of the sensible part of his brain.

Kara's teeth bit along her bottom lip as she toyed with his suggestion. 'Maybe I'm already going out somewhere? Maybe I have plans?'

Why wouldn't she? A beautiful woman like her was bound to have plans. 'Okay, well, that's fine. Another time.'

'I don't know…' She stared up at him through her long blonde fringe. 'I guess we should have a debrief, at least. Where would we go? Drake's?'

'Ah, no, after the day I've had I feel like taking a spin. A little farther, maybe? Somewhere I can breathe fresh air, away from the city. Blow out the cobwebs.'

'Not too far. I have an early morning start tomorrow, with a hell of a grumpy boss.'

Walking back to his bike, he handed her a helmet from the top box and grinned. It wasn't the early morning he was imagining…it was a late night…

Whoa, his libido was in super-drive. *Getting to know you* had suddenly got interesting.

Which was a pretty damned stupid idea, given she was already infiltrating his every thought. There were some guidelines he needed to be setting for himself too—e.g. a Kara-free life.

'Okay, so how about Hammersmith? There's a little pub there down on the water's edge, just near Furnival Gardens. Not quite Darling Harbour, I guess, but it's a decent spot and shouldn't be too busy.'

She stopped and regarded his bike with a grimace. 'I don't do bikes.'

'You've got to be open to new experiences, Kara. It's how we grow as people. It's just a bit of fun. What have you got to lose?'

'Skin? I know enough about plastic surgery to never go on a motorbike. *Ever.*' Weighing the helmet in her hand, she eyed him suspiciously. 'Do you always carry a spare helmet?'

'Not always. Just so happens the luck fairies have been busy sprinkling again. I'll be careful—and besides, London traffic is so slow we won't get above twelve miles an hour. Come on. Live a little.' Climbing on, he gestured to the back of the bike. 'I promise not to bite…unless you want me to.'

'Oh, no…biting is way off-limits.'

But she held his gaze and he caught that flicker of desire, those green eyes probing deeper into his soul. And he didn't miss the catch in her voice, the breathy sigh. He wondered, briefly, what was within her limits…

'So, are you getting on or not?'

'Seeing as you asked so nicely. Good to see that chivalry's not dead.'

'Wait. Wear this.'

Shrugging out of his jacket gave him a second to rethink this whole scenario. Man, he needed his head looked at—inviting her out when he should have been going through the Hunter Clinic's quarterly accounts instead of pandering to Ethan's demands. But his friend had been right. The least Declan could do was to lay down some ground rules. A quick drink. A work chat. Then make sure she got home safely. That was chivalry. Not giving in to feral instincts.

Unlike his father, who had given in to too many of his own needs, leaving everyone else to deal with the fall-out of his selfishness.

And Declan was nothing like his father.

'It can get cold on the bike and wearing this is safer. Like I said—my lucky jacket.'

He wrapped the jacket round her shoulders, held it while she slid her arms into the sleeves. It dwarfed her willowy frame and she looked like a hot rock chick, not a surgeon. An image that zinged straight to his groin, sending ripples of heat shimmying through him. He flicked her hair out from the jacket collar and slipped the helmet over her head, tightening the strap under her chin, drawing on every reserve not to kiss that pouty mouth.

'Okay, you're good to go. Hold tight.'

He held her hand as she lifted one red shoe and straddled the back seat. Held his breath as she slid her hands around his waist.

And he prayed to the luck fairies that she wouldn't hold on too tight. That his body wouldn't betray him again by reacting to her touch. That he could keep control of his libido long enough to get her safely home. Alone.

CHAPTER FOUR

So MUCH FOR *professional distance*. Kara climbed up behind Declan and placed her hands tentatively on his waist. Then, too close for any kind of sensibility, she let go and held on to the back of the bike.

'Okay,' she shouted as her helmet tapped the back of his. 'Hammersmith!'

'I'll take the scenic route—give you a bit of a tour.'

He grinned, giving her the thumbs-up and gunning the engine. A quick jolt as he accelerated made her inhale sharply and instinctively grasp round his waist again.

Right round.

Now her sharp intake of breath wasn't purely surprise, but was infused with a good dose of fire as her hands slid over cotton that slid over muscle. Beneath her fingers she felt the outline of his abs, lean and taut. Her mouth watered. If she'd been crazy blurting out her stupid answers in Theatre, it was nothing to the foolhardiness of hugging against him as they whizzed through the streets of west London.

At the touch of her breasts against his back awareness flowed through her. Famous city land-marks passed her by in a blur. She thought she might have seen Kensington Gardens ablaze with flowers, the Royal Albert Hall and queues of peo-ple waiting outside, the dazzling array of trendy shops in Kensington High Street, but she defi-nitely saw the musculature of Declan's arms as he steered, the tightening of his thigh as they waited at lights, the dips and lines of his shoulderblades.

The traffic flowed remarkably well for rush hour, and he wove the motorbike expertly in and out of the lanes. The warm breeze rushed into her face. The powerful throb and roar of the engine as they sped along gave a power-punch to her chest. Declan was right—this was definitely the way to blow out cobwebs. Her heart thumped and her body ached, but the only thing she knew for sure was that once this ride had ended it would take a lot of convincing for her to get off.

Although not once had she felt any shift in

Declan's focus, any kind of reaction to her hands on his body. Maybe she was dreaming that there was a connection between them? Maybe he truly did just want a conversation about their caseload?

In which case she would be fine. She could do professional. She could definitely do hands-off— just as soon as they stopped. For now, though, she was content to hold on tight.

Then, in too few wonderful minutes, they were pulling up outside a beautiful but tiny Tudor-style pub on the banks of the River Thames. Hanging baskets dripped pink and scarlet flowers over mahogany balconies; a smattering of people sat at round tables outside.

He helped her off the bike and unclipped her helmet. 'There we go. Fun, yes?'

'Wow, yes.'

Although not necessarily in the way he was thinking. Her legs felt a little unsteady as she stood, and she didn't think it was all due to the bike.

'I love it. Nothing can beat it. Oh, wait—maybe riding back in the dark, seeing London all lit up.' He secured their helmets in the top boxes, then pointed right along the paved riverfront. 'Should we take a walk first? There's a little pier farther down I like to explore.'

'Oh? Okay.'

She turned to take in the rest of the sights. To their left the green iron latticework of the Hammersmith Bridge dominated the view back towards the city. On the slow-running water members of a rowboat team practised strokes under the watchful eye of their cox. They paused briefly and waved.

Kara waved back. 'Seems like a lot of hard work to me.'

He laughed. 'I prefer rugby myself, but there's a rowing club just down the way. This place gets busy at the weekends, with people hanging out watching boat races and the like.'

'Do you play? Rugby?'

'When I have the time. I play for an Irish club based in Kilburn.'

That explained the toned body she'd run her fingers over. She forced words through a suddenly dry throat. 'What position?'

'You know about rugby?'

How many hours had she stood on the touchline and watched Rob get battered and bruised?

How many years of bolstering his flailing ego when they were beaten? Too many to count. It wasn't a memory she wanted to conjure up—or relive.

'Not really.' She changed tack. 'Being a consultant, I thought you'd be more of a wine bar, white tablecloth and fancy grog kind of guy.'

'Grog?'

'Remind me to bring a phrasebook next time. Grog is what we Aussies call beer.'

'I see. It sounded like you had something stuck in your throat.' He laughed. 'I enjoy bars like Drake's, for sure. There's a good crowd in there and it's friendly enough. But sometimes I like a little anonymity—being where everyone knows all your business is like being back home.'

'Or on an army base. Or at boarding school. Both of which I've done.'

'And didn't enjoy, by the look on your face.' He started to wander down the shrub-lined path. Thyme and lavender scented the air. 'I also like to go to places I can pop into wearing my leathers if I see fit. Drake's doesn't really fit that bill.'

'I'm sure they wouldn't mind.' *I wouldn't.*

She sniffed the leather jacket. Got another lungful of Declan. Steadied her heart-rate.

Across the river Kara saw large oak trees, a sports field, people jogging. Next to her Furnival Gardens was in full late-summer bloom, the flowers a little faded now, but bright still, very pretty and so typically English. It was a long way from Sydney's exotic botanical gardens. With no large bats eyeing her suspiciously or flapping their great grey wings over her head. Now, *there* was a bonus.

Ah, Sydney… Her heart stuttered just a little. But she calmed it down again. This new life, so many miles away from the place she'd tried desperately to call home, was going to be stress-free. So long as she kept her heart out of her decision-making.

They walked on towards a cluster of brightly coloured houseboats adorned with a variety of quirky ornaments: gnomes, Buddha statues and pots and pots of flowers. A family of ducks waddled past and slipped into the water.

She breathed the scented air deeply and relaxed her shoulders. 'I can't believe we're still in the middle of London. The air seems fresher here—

better than the confines of the city and the hospital's disinfectant smell.'

'It's a good place to clear your head. Sometimes I sneak down here at lunchtime for a run, just to get perspective. It's my guilty secret.' He stopped and turned to face her, looked straight into her eyes. 'What's yours, Kara?'

Oh, God. She forced the still air into her lungs and swallowed deeply. He was looking at her the way he had at the ball. As if he wanted to kiss her. Right now. Suddenly she realised she wanted to be his guilty secret, and him to be hers. To kiss those lips. To curl into his arms.

Dragging her eyes away from his, she glanced downwards. 'Shoes. They're my guilty secret.'

'Ah, yes. Of course. Although there's not a lot secret about that pair. They scream for attention.' He grinned, clearly liking what he saw. 'You sure you can manage a walk in them?'

'Definitely.'

At that moment a jogger ran past and Kara stepped sideways to let him through. Her feet sank into damp grass, ruby-red heels and all. Unless she wanted to hobble across the lawn as if she had some kind of terrible affliction she needed to admit defeat.

'But I think I'll just take them off to save the heels from being ruined.'

He waited as she sat on a bench and unfastened one shoe, then twisted to do the other one. Her hands shook a little as she tried to undo it.

'Damn thing—the strap's caught...'

'Do you need help?'

And there he was, in front of her again, bending down and peeling the second shoe off, oh, so slowly, his hand on her foot, her ankle, her calf. Her abdomen squeezed at the briefest touch of his fingers on her skin, at the tender way he slid the shoe over her toes, his head dipped in concentration. She almost reached out to run her fingers through that mess of hair. To pull him to her and breathe him in fully. She wondered how the hell someone she barely knew could fire such sensations within her.

Then, as if he'd only just realised the intimacy of such an act, he jumped back and stuffed his hands into his pockets. 'Better now?'

So she'd just discovered that ankles were a definite erogenous zone. Wriggling her toes into the soft lush grass, she smiled. 'Yes. Thank you. Beautiful they may be—but, boy, they feel even better off.'

He laughed, sitting down on the grass opposite her. It seemed the man was at ease wherever he was—operating on complex surgeries in Theatre, in front of the media, roaring through town or sitting peacefully catching the dying rays of sunshine.

'You're as bad as Niamh. She's always buying the most ridiculous shoes—even ones that don't fit properly—just because they're *works of art*, as she calls them.'

'She has good taste, then.'

'Or more money than sense.'

'Niamh?' She knew she was treading on tricky ground here, but she asked anyway. 'Is she one of your sisters?'

'Yes. The oldest of the girls.'

'And then…?'

He shrugged.

She nodded for him to continue.

His smile was hesitant. 'Then there's Aoife, Briana and Roisin.' He counted them off on his fingers.

'I hope there won't be a test, because I'm so going to fail at remembering them all.' *Efor?* 'There's a lovely musical ring to the names. What do they all do?'

'Apart from get under my feet?'

'There you go again—saying the words, but your face is all soft and filled with affection.'

'Ach, no, I was just squinting because the sun's in my eyes.' He laughed again.

Laughter came easily to him. She liked that. Liked that he found the fun in things. After the past few years she'd struggled to find the fun in anything much, and when Rob had come home all they'd done was argue. But Declan's smile was contagious.

She relaxed into the conversation as he chatted about his family.

'Let me see…you sure you want to hear this?'

'Of course. Like I say, I always wanted to have brothers and sisters.'

'Okay…well, don't say I didn't warn you… Niamh's married and has four kids. Aoife's engaged, for the third time, and has a little one— Declan.' He winced. 'Yes, after me, and not after the hapless idiot who got her pregnant. He disappeared into the ether at the mere mention of a baby. That was a big drama, as you can imagine.'

'Having a baby is always a drama one way or another. And Bri... Bri...?'

'Briana's talking about a wedding next year. Hasn't even met the poor fella yet. And Roisin is causing trouble at Trinity College in Dublin, training to be a doctor.'

Like her big brother. It was all so very different from Kara's life. Declan belonged to something bigger than himself—something full and lively—and he clearly adored them all, regardless of what he said.

A big fist of loneliness curled into her gut. She breathed it away. No point in wishing. All her life she'd tried to fit somewhere—and she'd never found her place, or herself. She'd tried the marriage and profession bit—it hadn't worked because something had had to give and it had ended up being her relationship. Now she just focused on her job, being useful, saving lives, putting people back together again. Taking any further kind of risk with her heart was just not on her horizon.

'How on earth do you keep track of them all?'

'Niamh is an excellent communicator, unfortunately. I think she has me on speed dial.' He rolled his eyes. 'Then there's texts and social media—it doesn't matter where you hide, they can always find you somehow.'

She laughed. 'And your mum and dad? Where are they?'

'Mam still lives on the farm…or rather… Ah, look, never mind.' Dark storms clouded his face. 'My dad…he's gone.'

'I'm sorry.'

'Not dead…just gone.' He offered her his hand and pulled her from the seat, shaking off whatever ghosts flitted at the back of those brown eyes. 'Come on.'

There was more to his family life than he was letting on. Something wasn't quite right. She knew enough about him not to push, but she wanted to ask him about his father. But that would be prying and probably intrusive. She didn't want that in *her* life, so she wouldn't inflict it on someone she hardly knew.

'Now, are you hungry?' He picked up her shoes and put his arms out towards her. 'Shoes or piggyback?'

'Oh, you're really getting the hang of the chivalry thing.'

But she shook her head, imagining how easy it would be to allow some fun into their working relationship. Getting physically close to him again would only make her think or feel something she'd regret. She wouldn't trust her heart to anyone again. So resolutely no piggybacks. The journey home, slammed up against him on the motorbike, would be hard enough.

'Thanks, but I can manage.'

She kept her distance as she walked barefoot into the pub and upstairs to a window seat overlooking the river.

Declan sat opposite her, that sexy mouth teasing her resolve. 'So, Kara, are you planning on staying in Burns and Plastics? Which particular area are you thinking of specialising in?'

'To be honest, I don't know. I love it all, but I'm not sure yet as to exactly where I'd fit.'

'What made you choose it in the first place?'

'I was amazed by the army medics my mother worked with—seeing how they could change someone's life after extensive injury made me want to do the same. So I guess I lean more towards reconstruction than cosmetics.'

'You didn't want to follow your parents into the army?'

She laughed, imagining herself taking orders… and failing. 'God, no, that was never on the cards. I like dealing with clients from all walks of life and different scenarios.'

He took a sip of beer and watched her for a moment, his brown eyes peering deep. 'And has it lived up to your expectations so far?'

'Oh, like all aspects of medicine there's plenty of times when it's devastating and frustrating—'

'When patients don't make it, or don't want to comply? Or when you know the causes of their injuries were avoidable?' He shook his head. 'Believe me, I know.'

'But I still get that mad buzz when someone leaves in a better condition, both physically and mentally, than when they came in. There's not a lot that can beat the high of success.'

'Oh? Really?' Declan put down his beer and leaned across the table. 'Use your imagination, Kara. I can think of a few things.'

She didn't need to ask him what he meant.

Those eyes caught on hers again as he smiled, slow and lazy. Sexy too. Very, *very* sexy. An unspoken buzz fizzed between them. Something that was intangible but clear.

Again with the blushing. She couldn't remember Rob ever making her blush, or making her feel this weird mix of fear and excitement just by talking. She wanted to touch Declan. To smooth down that unruly mop of hair. To feel the rough edges of his jaw against her palm, her cheeks, her mouth.

Oh, boy.

'Anyway, am I still on the team, then?' she asked, trying to keep a work focus as the waiter brought their food—a Thai chicken salad for herself and steak for Declan.

In between bites of the most succulent lemongrass-marinated chicken she'd ever tasted she chatted on.

'Do I meet your extremely high standards?'

'I guess I can put up with you. You seem to have exemplary surgical skills and an uncanny knack of knowing what I need even before I do. Which is weird...but I can live with it.' His mouth twitched. 'So we do indeed have an early start tomorrow. I want to check in on Safia before our surgery list starts—make sure she's coping with the pain and the new dressings. Then we're over at the Hunter Clinic to review a couple of private clients in the afternoon. Somewhere in between you can regale the team again with your exploits in Sydney.'

Her cheeks remained heated. 'I'm sorry about that. I don't usually talk about my private life in the middle of an operation.'

'That's a very good policy to adopt. There's a wicked gossip machine here and it can get you into all kinds of trouble. I find it's best to try to keep a private life well away from work. It stops things getting messy.'

'And who needs messy?'

Messy didn't begin to describe her marriage—it had started out so beautiful, so…naive. Messy had only begun somewhere about the time she'd determined she was going to study full-time, and messy had certainly come to full iridescent bloom at the funeral service.

She gave Declan a tight smile. He was renowned for keeping his relationships clinical. Short. Uncomplicated. And if ever she was going to have sex again that was her game plan too—but he definitely didn't figure in her picture of casual sex partner. Sleeping with the boss would be messy and then some.

She knew better too than to get into a conversation about anything other than work, but she'd muddied things by blurting out details of her life in the middle of an operation. She really did need to make sure he knew that kiss had been fully consensual, and had nothing to do with her memories of Rob or loneliness. And that it wouldn't happen again.

'I like to keep things as uncomplicated as possible. My focus is wholly on my job and I can't see that changing any time soon.' She took a large drink of wine and steadied herself. 'I should tell you, though, just to be clear, that my husband died.'

She could say the whole sentence now without the catch in her voice. She'd come a very long way.

Declan's eyes widened and he put his glass down. 'Oh, God, I never thought… Divorce, perhaps. Separation. What the hell happened?'

'He was killed in action in Afghanistan. Full

military honours funeral—quite the hero.' She fought back the rising feelings of guilt, loss and sheer disbelief that had rocked through her for so long. This new start of hers included leaving the sadness behind too. Although that was so much harder to achieve than she'd thought.

'So he was in the army too?'

'Yes. I spent the best part of my teens rebelling against it, but ended up marrying into the firm after all. It was all I ever knew, really. I was very young—too young at eighteen—and I wanted the whole wedding fairytale. Oh, and a career and a family too. Just like every other girl I know.'

She thought back to the struggles they'd both had adjusting to married life, reasserting their individual dreams and trying to mesh them somehow so they could both be fulfilled and happy. She'd wanted a place where she could belong. Finally. Truth was she hadn't found it with Rob either.

Declan's hand covered hers. 'I'm so sorry, Kara. How long ago did he die?'

'Eighteen months.'

He did the maths. 'So the hospital ball must have been close to—?'

'The year anniversary. Yes.' She drew her hand away from his and watched him frown. She didn't want his pity or his sympathy; she just wanted to clear the air. Then she could move on. *Again.* 'But I think I know where you're going with this… Rob dying was devastating, and I'm not sure I'll ever be the same again, but that kiss you and I shared had nothing to do with him. Seriously.'

Declan ran his fingers across his scalp. There were times when she knew exactly what he was thinking. There were times too when he became closed-off and distant. Right now she wasn't sure what he was thinking at all.

'Yes, Kara, about that kiss…'

CHAPTER FIVE

FINALLY THAT PARTICULAR ghoul was out of its box. Its spectre had hung over them for the best part of twenty-four hours. Or, in reality, six months.

As she put her knife and fork down and sat back in her chair the shadows under Kara's eyes melted away a little. 'It was a mistake,' she asserted.

'Hmm…' Declan disagreed with her. 'Losing your car keys is a mistake. Getting drunk and disorderly is a mistake. Kissing someone like that is no mistake.'

'Well, okay, it was just downright foolish. And it can never happen again.'

'No.'

But, heck, he wanted it to—even now. Even after hearing about the heartbreak she'd been through. She was over the death of her husband? The army hero? *Yeah, right.* Declan knew that loss never left you; the pain dimmed over time, sure, but it still ached in your bones, resurfaced at moments you didn't expect. It snatched clean away the ability to be carefree and left a distrust that life could ever be the same.

But she was clear that their kiss and her mourning her husband's death were separate—perhaps that was what she wanted to believe.

That night at the ball she'd been soft and yet sharp in his arms, vulnerable and yet defiant as she'd laughed and joked and drunk and danced. And very, *very* sexy. There were layers to her—a fractured beauty about her that intrigued him.

He didn't know how to react to this. Was it wrong to want her after everything she'd been through?

It would be wrong to follow through, he decided—she'd been hurt enough, and he wasn't the kind of man to give her what she needed. But even so he ached to finish what they'd started. The more time he spent with her the more he wanted to kiss her again. And again. To take things to their natural conclusion—bed. Because he could do that very easily.

It was the rest of it—the promises and com-

mitment, the *love* he couldn't do. After the heartbreak he'd seen his mother go through he would
never make himself weak and vulnerable—never
leave his heart open to such hurt.

So he usually had fun with women who were
on the same page as him. Not women who had
already had one long-term, this-is-for-life relationship and who clearly deserved another. With
the right man. Not him.

'No. You're right. It can't happen again.' That
was the right thing to do. The sensible part of his
brain cheered from the sidelines.

She flicked her hand nonchalantly. 'We have
to work together.'

'Yes.'

'And you're my boss.'

'Yes.'

'And...' Her eyebrows knotted. She obviously couldn't think of another reason why they
shouldn't kiss again.

Even though he thought he might be able to persuade her to the contrary, he put his own wants
aside. 'And I don't do relationships. And you just
came out of one.'

'Hardly. It was a long time ago.'

'You're still hurting. That much is obvious.'

'I'm not. But you don't have to convince me, you know. I *do* get it. We're not doing anything again.'

She looked stung by his words.

'And, yes, Rob's death knocked me for six, that's for sure, but I am in control of my emotions now. I was totally in control back then at the ball too.'

'Knocking back shots was fully in control? Man, I'd love to see you let loose.' She'd been intent on getting wasted and had invited him to join her. Which he had done quite happily, until… 'So why kiss me then run away?'

'Let's just say that in a dim attempt to forget what the occasion was—i.e. the anniversary of Rob's death—I had decided tequila would be the memory-eraser of choice. And I was having a jolly time. Great company.' She winked. 'But suddenly, in a blinding flash of sobriety, I realised that instead of impressing my new bosses I was snogging one of them. And that anything more would be a really bad idea.' Finally her mouth curved into a smile and she pointed at him. '*You* were a bad idea.'

Still no mention of the sizzling static that had crackled between them. The same sizzle that snapped in the air between them now, like a firecracker.

Kiss me.

Oh, yes, he wanted to. '*I* was a bad idea? That's new.'

The smile played along her lips as her eyes brightened. 'Well, you've got to be open to new experiences, Declan. That's how we grow as people.'

'Oh, and we have a comedian in the building. Very clever, Ms Stephens.'

'What's the matter? Is your ego having trouble reconciling that you weren't who I wanted to spend the rest of that night with?'

'My ego is thoroughly intact...' He leaned towards her, unable to resist the allure of that smile. 'Because I don't believe you. You want to know what I think?'

'Not really,' she said

She was smirking in that sarcastic way girls had that was strangely sexy and infuriating at the same time. If she'd been one of his sisters he'd have been hard pushed not to tap her cute ass.

'Oh, do go on. The suspense is killing me.'

'I think you wanted that kiss as much as I did. And that you wonder just what might have happened...'

'I know exactly what would have happened.'

And he could see that she was heading the same way right now too. They both were. Dangerous enough for a fledgling work team. Even more so for a woman whose heart had been shattered and for a man who had no heart left to give. So what the hell his wayward mouth was doing, flirting and teasing, he didn't know.

But he just couldn't help it. 'You never thought about a re-run?'

'Never.'

Her eyes met his and despite her words to the contrary the truth shimmered there in pupils as green as the fields back home.

Home. Reality hit. 'Okay, we should probably be going. Have you finished? Where do you live? I'll give you a lift back.'

'Shepherds Bush.'

She told him the address and for a moment he thought about asking her who else lived there. Did she have flatmates? Was she on her own?

Did she need company? He wasn't used to dropping and running. He was used to the sweet magic of commitment-free sex and the unspoken agreement that it was a one-night thing. But not pushing Kara for anything more felt respectful, right…and way out of his comfort zone. It seemed there were a lot of things about this Aussie whirlwind that sent him off-kilter.

He led her out, helped her on with the helmet, watched as she again sheathed her body in his jacket, washing it in her own sweet perfume. He climbed onto his seat and held his breath as she settled in behind him. This time she didn't hesitate to wrap her arms around his waist.

Many times he'd given rides to his sisters and their friends, to colleagues and to dates. Many times a woman had wrapped her hands around his waist but he had never felt so twitchy and so hot. *Damned* hot.

Kara's legs straddled his back. Those shoes either side of his bike were like some goddamned teenage fantasy. Her breathing was sketchy and shallow, her heat fused to his skin and his hormones hit red alert. Gripping the handlebars as if his life depended on them, he accelerated into the night-time traffic, hoping that the brief journey and the night air would cool things down.

No such luck. When he pulled up outside her apartment his gut swirled with a mixture of relief and regret. Laughing, she grabbed his hand and wiggled off the seat, rocking slightly on those take-me-to-bed heels as she straightened up.

So she didn't have to struggle further, he unclipped her helmet and brushed down her hair. The kind of thing he'd do any time for Niamh or Roisin. But the way his groin tightened at Kara's sexy smile of thanks was anything but brotherly.

After he'd removed his own helmet he ventured a question that he hoped she'd refuse. He needed to get away, and fast. 'Do you want me to come up with you, or wait here until you're safely inside?'

'Thanks, Declan, but you go home. I can manage. I'm a big girl now.' She found a key in her bag and paused on the steps up to the grandiose Georgian facade of newly refurbished apartments. 'Thanks heaps for the meal and the bike ride. It was fun.'

'No problem. See you tomorrow. Nice and early.'

He made himself turn around, forced the next few steps away from her, but when he reached his motorbike he felt the soft weight of her hand on his shoulder.

Caught the hitch in her breath.

Heard her whisper once more. 'Kiss me...'

'Kara...'

Her name on his lips sent hot sensations skittering through her abdomen and down her shaking legs. God knew what she was saying or doing, but she couldn't let him go without tasting him again. Could not breathe him in, feel the pressure of his body between her legs on that motorbike, could not hold him tight against her and then *not* feel that mouth on hers.

She'd lied. She'd thought about a re-run of that kiss too many times to count. And now she was going to make it happen. Because if she didn't she might just die. Was it possible to die of desire?

He turned, his look of shock similar to the way he'd reacted to her at the ball. The message in his heated pupils was the same too.

He palmed her cheek and smiled. 'What happened to never again?'

'Never say never.'

Her hands found their way to his jacket collar as she lifted her mouth to his before her courage left her. For a moment she thought he was going to resist or reject her, that maybe she'd read all those signs woefully wrong, but then he pressed his lips against hers, his hands framing her face, his touch heart-meltingly tender.

He tasted of something exciting, of adventure, and of a mysterious heat that seeped into her skin. This was nothing like the kiss they'd shared at the ball—this was deeper, sexier and filled with six months' worth of wishing, of relentless holding back and scorching dreams.

'God, Kara.'

His hands ran down her back as he pressed against her, his heart beating a raging tattoo that matched every beat of hers. And even when she knew this was the most foolish thing to do she pressed harder against him. Even when she knew that this was going nowhere she slid her tongue into his mouth, heard the groan in his throat, smiled as his breathing quickened.

She brushed her foot against his leg and he groaned again, in that deep voice that reached into her insides and stroked. 'Those are the sexiest damned shoes I have ever seen. Whatever happens, do not take them off.'

'Aye-aye, sir.' She wiggled against his hips, leaving him in no doubt as to her intentions.

The energy around them was supercharged. The kiss became hotter and more urgent. It was the kind of kiss that you searched for the whole of your life and rarely did you ever find it. Unexpected, exciting. Perfect.

She ran her fingers over his back, down to the waistband of his jeans, and pulled him closer, arcing her body to fit to his, feeling the swell of hardness between them. His mouth was on her neck now, tracing a soft trail to her shoulder, nibbling, teasing, biting.

Her fingers bunched in that scruffy mop of hair as her breasts pressed against him, her nipples hardening as they brushed against his body. Sensation after sensation rippled through her as his hand swept across her ribs, over her bra. Under her bra. Right there on the city street. And then he was sitting her on the motorbike, steadying himself in front of her, his legs straddling hers.

This was the most sexy, the most alive she'd felt in too long. The most amazing. The most thrilling. And if they didn't stop soon they'd be making love on that black and chrome steel.

Was she crazy?

Yes. She probably was. But she needed this, needed him, needed a night when she could be a sexy woman instead of a grieving widow. When she could feel and be held and be wanted. When she could take what she wanted, be herself instead of trying to fit into someone else's mould. Where she could have Declan Underwood in her bed.

She put some space between them—just enough so she could speak. Her hands didn't leave his body; her eyes didn't leave his face. She barely recognised her own voice, 'Do you want to come upstairs? For...?'

He stilled and closed his eyes for a second, knowing that coffee was not on the menu. When he opened them again she knew his answer before he even said the words.

'I should go.'

No. 'But—' The heat coursing through her veins ran cold with embarrassment and disappointment. He didn't want this after all—didn't want her. And she'd made yet another fool of herself in front of her boss.

His palms stroked over her shoulders. 'Go, Kara. Go now, before we do something we'll both regret.'

'Right. Thanks.' Rubbing a hand across her swollen mouth, she held back the sarcastic laugh. She didn't think she could ever regret spending the night with him.

'You know what I mean. We agreed this would be very unwise. Look, I'm not easy to get on with. I don't answer calls. I don't make promises. I'm not there when I'm needed. Except in my job. I'm always there for my job. The truth is, you don't need me in your life.'

'It was just a kiss, Declan.' Although she got the feeling that their kiss was just the tip of the breath-sapping, heart-stopping, wet and wild iceberg.

'And very nearly something else.'

He gave her a wavering smile. Not a let's-get-naked smile. Not a promising-three-times-a-night kind of smile. The kind of smile, she suspected, he gave his patients before he broke bad news. Or the kind of smile he'd given to one of his sisters when the pet goldfish died. It was not the smile she wanted.

'Go to bed. I'll see you tomorrow. Nice and early.'

And before she could answer he'd pulled on his motorbike helmet and disappeared into the night. Leaving her hot and definitely bothered and with no clue how she was going to face him in the morning.

She needn't have worried. He was far too engrossed in his work to bother about the events of the previous night.

They stood in a large group in Safia's room, trying to get the teenager to vent her feelings. No such luck.

Clean-shaven, hair wrangled into smart submission, and wearing a dark charcoal suit, crisp white shirt and silver-grey tie, Declan looked as if he'd stepped out of the cover of a magazine. Kara remembered how his rough jaw had felt across her cheek, how he'd smelt of leather and heat, the way he'd tasted of adventure, the way he'd whispered her name into the night. How his eyes had blazed with a heat that had threatened to engulf her.

Today, however, he looked rested, calm and perfectly unaffected. Kara, on the other hand, was well aware she had dark smudges under her eyes from a restless night. From dreams about getting hot and heavy under sheets of a substantially lower thread count than the Sheikha was used to.

His voice was soft as he spoke to their client. 'So, Safia, how are you feeling today?'

Dressed in casual clothes, rather than her country's traditional heavily jewelled dress, the young girl sat in a chair and stared out of the window, her arms elevated for optimum healing. So far this morning she'd refused to speak or even to look at the surgical team. Thick tears ran down her face and she made no attempt to stop them.

Kara relayed what she'd learnt from the nursing staff earlier that morning, 'Safia didn't have a great night. She reports having little pain, but she's…well, she's generally not having the best of days. Temperature's fine, though. Bloods are normal. There's no sign of infection. Physically she's making good progress.'

'Ach, Safi...' Declan drew up a chair and sat next to her. 'Everything is going well. So what's the matter?'

'You wouldn't understand.'

'No? Try me.'

He ushered out the attending nurses, the medical students, the physio and even the Sheikha's parents. Kara waited for an indication of what he wanted her to do—stay or leave. God, a re-run of the night before.

This time nothing flashed behind those eyes that made her feel she should be embarrassed, but there was no reassurance there either. He was nothing but the consummate professional. Heat rose to her cheeks and she picked up her papers and made for the door.

What the hell had she been thinking?

Nothing. She'd thought of nothing past touching her mouth to his, being wrapped in those arms. Nothing about her responsibilities to the team, to Ethan, to her patients. To her job. To everything she'd sacrificed. She'd been willing to throw all that aside and give in to temptation without a thought for the next minute, never mind the next day, just to have one more kiss with Declan.

Well, it wouldn't happen again.

Out in the corridor a nurse stopped and asked Kara to sign a prescription chart. Then a patient's relative asked for an update. Seemed everyone wanted to talk to her except Declan.

She turned for one quick look back into Safia's room and something about the way he was sitting close to his patient, his voice so gentle, rooted Kara to the spot.

He leaned close and took the girl's hand, looking out across the city and not directly at Safia. A ploy, Kara thought, not to stress the girl out by focusing on her too intently, but to cajole her somehow into talking.

'I see a lot of things in this job, Safia. I see people who have survived terrible accidents, who have lost everything except the ability to haul breath into smoke-damaged lungs. And some are not even capable of that. I see carelessness that leads to injury and I see beautiful people who believe they can't go on but who still have the rest of their lives to live, somehow. And it makes me sad.'

'So why do you do it?' The Princess blinked and wiped her bandaged fist across her eyes, wrestling control over the sobs that had racked her chest. 'Why don't you do something else for a job? Although don't try singing—you do really suck at that.'

'Yeah, I know. Liam's job is safe for now. Truth is, there's nothing else I want to do.' He smiled and turned to her. 'Because when someone can't stay strong for themselves they need someone else to help them along. I kind of see myself as doing that. I stay strong for you until you can find the strength in yourself.' He shrugged. 'Oh, and it just so happens that I'm a genius with a scalpel too. That definitely helps.' He winked at her. 'You're doing fine, Safia. You *will* be fine. This is the hardest bit, you know. Coming to terms with it all.'

'I don't want to come to terms. I want it to have not happened at all.'

He shook his head. 'Ah, sweetheart, I know you do. I know how hard it is. Trust me, I know.'

'How? How do you know? You're a doctor. You're not burned. You don't look like...this.'

Kara squeezed a folder to her chest and watched as emotion bled from his face.

But he didn't shy away from Safia's question. Instead he ran a hand across the back of his neck and nodded. 'Okay...I don't tell everyone this, but it might help you. I hope it does...' He inhaled sharply. 'When I was thirteen we had a fire at our house. I got the little ones out safely, but I just couldn't get to my mammy—my mum—in time...and she got burnt, like you, on her face and her hands...'

Oh, God. Kara's heart thumped and squeezed. She imagined Declan as a young, innocent kid, fighting to save the lives of his family, going back into a burning house to save them. How utterly terrifying.

Blinking back tears, she focused on the blurry piece of paper in front of her. *'Temperature normal. Blood pressure within normal limits...low mood...healing well...'*

Her own reasons for becoming a surgeon paled into the background as she learnt the real reason he fought every day to save people, to try to piece them back together again. And every day the horror of that fire must be somewhere in his mind, spurring him on. She imagined he'd almost lost them in the black smoke and the heat, and realising he hadn't managed to save his mother from being hurt must have bitten deep.

For a man like Declan that would have been a failure. But instead of running away from those demons he forced himself to face them every day.

But he was in London, not back home in Ireland. Had he moved here so he didn't have to face her every day instead? And what about his father? Declan hadn't mentioned him. Hadn't mentioned his dad's role in all of this.

So many questions buzzed around her head.

'So what happened after that?' Safia's voice had lost a little of its self-pity as she stared into Declan's face. 'Is she okay now?'

'She spent a lot of time in hospital and she was very troubled by everything that happened and more. They were hard times, Safia. How she looked on the outside greatly affected how she felt on the inside.'

He waited until the ramifications of that statement settled on Safia's face.

112 200 HARLEY STREET: THE SHAMELESS MAVERICK

'She wouldn't do her physio, she wouldn't try any more treatments, so her hands and fingers got stiff and sore. She basically lost the strength to carry on. For a long time she let her appearance and her residual pain rule her life.'

Safia's eyebrows rose. 'That's very sad.'

'Yes, it was. She struggled to find that strength within her to make the best of things. That's why I have to be strong, eh?'

He gave her the kindest smile Kara had ever seen.

'But you've got the whole of your life to look forward to. You have very important things to do—I know this—and a happy life to grasp. You *will* get through this, Safia, believe me. You will get through this with dignity and grace and you will make a wonderful life for yourself.'

And until she could he would be there for her... being strong when she couldn't find strength within herself.

Small wonder the young girl looked up at him now with something akin to adoration. 'I'll try.'

'Promise me?'

'Yes. Yes, I promise.' It was a small voice but a big victory.

Kara breathed out slowly. It seemed that the more she learnt about Declan Underwood, the more involved she wanted to become. So she was grateful that he'd stopped talking, because if he was as damaged as she thought he was—and even half as damaged as she was—she could open herself up to a whole new world of hurt.

He turned and caught Kara standing there watching. His mouth opened in surprise, then tightened into a thin line. A torrent of emotion swam across his gaze and solidified into anger.

'Ms Stephens?'

'Yes? Sorry. I…er…' She wanted to tell him she hadn't heard, but he knew she had—knew she'd been listening to him bare his soul. And that, she surmised, was like rubbing his wound raw again.

Then he shook his head and with that swift action flicked the anger off. His shoulders were smoothed down, his features took on their normal ridges and planes.

'Okay, Safia, so we'll be back later to see how you're doing. In the meantime I'll send the physiotherapist in and you can start some gentle exercises to help regain the range of movement in that hand. Now, Ms Stephens, we have a surgery to do.'

'Yes, of course.'

Kara hurried in front of him and headed to the operating theatre, where she could bury herself deeper in her job and forget about the red-hot desire burning through her. Forget about the flash of pain and his subsequent refusal to acknowledge it.

Then, when she was finished for the day, she would work out the best way to stop herself from falling headlong into disaster.

CHAPTER SIX

'YOU WANT TO request a transfer? Are you mad?' Declan exhaled long and hard. Now his day was definitely going to the dogs. His day *never* went to the dogs. Work was the one thing he could control in his life: easy, predictable, calm.

He couldn't help thinking this downward trajectory had all started with the appearance of a certain Kara Stephens. The way she'd looked at him after he'd spoken about his mother... God, such pity in those green eyes. He didn't do this— didn't open up old wounds, didn't want sympathy. Never.

Damn. What was she doing to him? What the hell was *he* doing?

He didn't want drama. And no doubt that was what he'd have got if he'd blathered on any longer. That and memories causing a fist of pain under his ribcage.

He'd been trying to help a young girl, not much

younger than his sisters, who reminded him of their feisty spirit, who had got under his skin a little. And along with helping her he'd blown open the secrets of his heart.

Damn. Damn.

So much for escaping to London and putting his troubles behind him.

He glared over the sleek smoky glass desk in his Hunter Clinic office, barely able to comprehend what Kara was saying. Or to reconcile his rapid tachycardia and the thud in his stomach as she spoke in that cute accent that dipped and rose like the County Dublin hills.

'I know it's going to be difficult and will leave you short-staffed, Declan, but I just thought it might be better if I went back to my old team.'

'You're out of your mind.' But, really, he must have been too, to have kissed her back so completely. So totally and completely. And to be sitting here now, wanting to do it again regardless of the fact she'd seen him raw and open.

He didn't want her to leave. Okay, to be brutally honest, he wanted to have her, here in his plush white and light office. To slowly peel off her cream silky top, to strip off her tight black skirt…leaving the beige heels on, though… Man, his thoughts were X-rated…

He was at *work*, goddamn it.

He leant back in his chair. It had been a long day of holding back and he was reaching the end of his self-control. 'So why do you want to transfer?'

'Because of last night.'

'You want to leave because of one kiss?'

'Two kisses, actually.'

She held up two fingers, as if to ram home the point. A lesser woman would blush or shy away from the subject, but this was Kara and it seemed she always tackled things head-on. He thought he saw a smile waiting in the background there too, in the slight twitch of her mouth and a startling sparkle in her eyes. But then it was gone, replaced by steel.

'Two. Kisses.' She shook her head. 'I kissed you twice.'

'I know. I mastered counting single numbers in reception class. Personally, I thought they were pretty damned good.'

He rested his chin on his hands as his eyes met hers. If this wasn't such a serious conversation he could have some fun here. Hell, it had been hard enough to walk away yesterday and now here she was, trying to make it easier for him, and all he could think of was that he wanted more. A lot more. A lot more of everything. Particularly those slender legs, that tight nip of a waist. That cocky, forthright mouth.

What the hell was happening to him? She made a mockery of his self-control and a challenge to every promise he'd ever made to himself about getting in too deep.

'But a kiss is definitely not something I'd want to leave my job over.'

'I would hardly be leaving my *job*. It's just a sideways move to a different consultant and team. Don't get me wrong, Declan, the kisses were great. But I think we're struggling to draw a line here. This is work, our jobs…we can't stuff that up. If I go and work with someone else then we can put a stop to this…*kissing thing.*'

'Whoa…so, let me get this right. You want to leave me high and dry, with no junior surgeon and a heavy caseload, at the beck and call of a royal family, with a frightened patient who has developed a great rapport with you…' God forgive him for using Safia in this '…just because we had a kiss? In our free time? As consenting adults?'

'Two kisses. And I'm trying to do the right thing. The professional thing. What happens if this…attraction spills over to work? We can't afford to let it distract us.'

It was too late for that. And why he suddenly felt a need to defend their actions he didn't know.

'It won't. People have work liaisons all the time and it doesn't interfere with their ability to do their job.'

'No? Do you want to kiss me now?'

He checked his watch. 'It's after five and we're not technically required to be here… And you're an attractive woman. Any man would want to kiss you.'

'Not helpful. We're supposed to be having a meeting. At work.' She frowned. 'Safia is almost headed in the right direction now, so she doesn't need me, and besides it's you she has the real rapport with anyway. I'm sure they can find a replacement. I'll swap with someone. There are plenty of doctors who'd jump at the chance of working with you.'

'But you're not one of them.'

Her shoulders slumped forward. 'Of course I am, and I've loved every minute of it. But, come on, Declan. We both have jobs to do and this could get in the way. This…this is crazy.'

And the rest. He never spent more than a few minutes thinking about a woman. His life had no space for this. His heart certainly didn't.

Fun, yes—a little playful, harmless fun. But nothing more. And with Kara he had a feeling she wanted more. With what she'd been through she certainly deserved more.

'And if you do leave? Then what?'

She held her hand up. 'I just want to put a huge wedge of space between me and temptation. My life's been stuffed up too many times already.'

Which wasn't exactly a ringing endorsement of his kissing talent. He should have been relieved. He wasn't.

'I have to warn you that my first impulse is to say no. Things aren't going well for Karen's mum and she's requested further time off. If you transfer out it will leave the clinic in difficulty.'

'Oh. I see.'

'Look, I need a good junior surgeon and I have

one. Why would I give that up for the sake of temptation? I don't intend to allow my work to be compromised.'

His private desires could go to hell. Was it really because he would be short-staffed? Or was it because he was being selfish? *Gah,* he hated that thought—that he would use his needs to make someone do something they didn't want to.

If that was the case he was no better than his deadbeat father, who had fed his own pathetic needs before putting food in his kids' mouths, forcing a boy to do the work of a man. Who had betrayed the love of his family, his wife. His son.

So, no, he didn't want to be selfish—but he also didn't want to be short-staffed to the point that something had to give. With the desperate needs of his patients and the reputation of the clinic in his hands he had too much at stake right now.

He bit down on the flare of heat as she glared at him. A challenge. But not, he suspected, with the kind of result she was expecting. Because instead of annoying him it fired him.

'Okay, well, leave it with me. I have an urgent report to write in what's left of this evening. I'll see you in the morning. We can talk more then.'

Scraping his chair back, he stood and walked to her side of the desk. She stood too, picked up her bag and slung it across her body—a very chic leather barrier. Slamming down the venetian blinds, he turned to her, watched the steel in her pupils melt into hazy heated green.

She could have left. For that matter so could he. But the only direction his feet moved in was towards her.

He ran his fingers through a loose curl of her hair, reached out and pulled the messy ponytail down until her blonde hair pooled over her shoulders. Then he grasped a handful of it and breathed in the sweet scent of freedom and heat.

He looked into her face, at the smattering of freckles over her nose, her perfect full lips glistening with a pale, barely there lip-gloss, then into those eyes that searched his soul. His thumb ran a trail down her cheek, landed on her mouth, and she bit gently down on the soft pad and smiled. His groin tightened as spasms of heat shimmied through him.

She gasped, but she didn't pull away. 'Two kisses, Declan...'

And both times she'd asked him. Now it was his turn.

He leaned into her neck and whispered, 'Kiss me.'

And he could tell by the way her body softened towards him that she did want that. More than anything. That this buzz between them tugged hard, and that she was struggling to fight it. But he didn't wait—couldn't wait—to do what he'd been aching to do since he'd forced himself to walk away last night. He lowered his mouth onto hers, felt the hesitation, the sharp intake of breath, then felt the heat and the need spiral through her.

She wound her hands around his neck as the kiss deepened. And he should have stopped. He should have allowed her to go, to walk away from his team and to stop this *kissing thing...* But he couldn't. Something about Kara Stephens made him want to hold on and never let go.

A sharp knock at the door had them jumping apart. Kara stepped away from Declan on jelly legs and hung on to the back of a chair, her grip as white as the expensive upholstery. She didn't want to look at him, but she stole a glance to see how he was reacting.

Instead of being in any way embarrassed or flustered, like her, he looked triumphant as he held up three fingers. 'Three. Kisses.'

Kiss number three had *so* not been in her plan.

What was it about him that made her want to kiss him so thoroughly? And so many times?

His story and his humility had touched something deep inside her and that reaction had frightened her. The only logical thing she could do, she'd thought, was to move away…not kiss him again. Every contact she had with him dragged her deeper and deeper under his spell. This wasn't just about a purely physical attraction, and that realisation scared her more than anything.

Her cheeks and body ablaze, she inhaled and searched for inner serenity as Ethan Hunter walked into the room. When all she could find was inner chaos she gave up and threw the head of the Hunter Clinic's charitable arm a wobbly smile, hoping that, if nothing else, she could at least project a semblance of calm. 'Hi, Ethan.'

'Kara, hello. How are you?'

She'd heard rumours about Ethan's temper and

mood swings, but so far her dealings with him had been only professional. However, well used to being around army veterans, she could spot the invisible wounds, the need to be treated equally, especially after being damaged both emotionally and physically—as Ethan had been—and the refusal to accept any weakness.

Although he clearly believed he hid them well, Ethan wore the scars in his limp and in his stubborn refusal to use a walking stick, and in his absolute unwavering dedication to his reconstructive work on wounded soldiers and war victims alike.

It had been Ethan's suggestion that she join Declan's team, so now would be a good time to mention that she'd like a transfer...and then start tomorrow as far away from Declan as physically possible. But as she opened her mouth to speak her courage flailed and then collapsed in a puddle.

Was leaving the team the right thing to do? Or should she just wrestle her stupid wayward emotions into some kind of order? Was she just a wobbling mess of overreaction?

'I...er...I'm good, thanks.'

Ethan gave her a small smile. 'Thanks for moving across to work with Declan's team. You helped us out of a big hole there.' He nodded towards Declan. 'He has a lot on his plate, holding the fort here while Leo's away, on top of his workload and other commitments. Lucky for us he knows just how to pander to royals.'

'I like them. They're just as frightened as the rest of us when it comes to surgery, and they all need our help. Besides, Safia can't help her background. Kara's been great with her, though—settled her down…got her to open up…' Declan grinned, fully aware of Kara's discomfort. 'I don't know what I'd do without her if she left. Anyway, what can I do for you, Ethan?'

Declan offered him a seat, which he ignored. 'A drink?'

Ethan glanced over to the decanters but shook his head. 'No, thanks. I just wanted to have a quick chat about cover for Mitchell and Grace's leave… As you know, their wedding's coming up so we'll be two more surgeons down, leaving us short-staffed to cover on-call responsibilities at the clinic. If anyone else goes we'll be in big trouble.'

Declan turned to Kara and raised his eyebrows. 'Actually, Kara was just saying—'

'That I'm more than happy to stay on until Karen gets back.'

She threw Declan a look that she hoped would convey how frustrated she felt. What was the use in arguing? Clearly there was a lot riding on her placement here, and creating personnel issues wouldn't leave them well disposed to writing her a good reference.

And who in their right mind would walk away from working at the glamorous Hunter Clinic? Its client list was a who's-who in movie world cosmetic surgery, and Ethan's charity work brought in heartbreaking yet challenging cases from war-torn areas. As a place to hone her craft it was the very best in the world. It was too good an opportunity to give up just because of a kiss.

Three kisses.

Three kisses going nowhere. She was over trying to save things that were going nowhere. Like her marriage. And as it looked as if she was stuck working with Declan she'd keep her heart well out of it. She could do that.

She could.

* * *

A flurry of footsteps tapping on the marble floor out in the corridor had them all turning towards the door. Kara breathed out, grateful for the added distraction.

'Here you all are! Makes a change for me to be crashing into someone else's room.'

The Hunter Clinic head, Leo Hunter, stalked in, wearing a huge grin. Following right behind, her hand firmly in her new husband's grip, came Lizzie.

'Thought you'd all be home by now—it's getting late.'

'Just catching up on things.' Declan strode over and shook his friend's hand warmly. 'Good to see you. Good honeymoon? Or shouldn't I even ask?'

'Great. I think it was France, right? Didn't get out much…far too busy…' Leo winked as he shared the joke with Declan, but then his smile slipped a little as he looked over to his brother, Ethan, who cautiously smiled back. 'Hello, Ethan.'

'Hi, Leo. Lizzie.' Ethan walked over, his face serious and his shoulders hitched. He grazed his sister-in-law's cheek with a hurried kiss, shook his brother's hand quickly, then stepped away.

Kara watched with interest as the family dynamics came in to play. With his broad smile and easy manner Leo was clearly pleased to be back at the clinic he'd worked so hard to salvage from scandal and near ruin. Whereas Ethan's response was...*guarded* to say the least.

Again, the gossip machine had informed her of the rift between the brothers that was slowly healing but was not quite mended yet. For two people so passionately involved in putting lives back together they had resolutely failed to fix their own. There had been difficult scenes, terrible arguments and times when the brothers had clashed spectacularly. But after Ethan had been best man for Leo and Lizzie's wedding there had been some new, more friendly ground covered. Although, as far as Kara could see, the smile Ethan gave them still didn't quite reach his eyes.

Declan stepped forward and kissed Lizzie's cheek too. Warmth emanated from his smile. The contrast between him and Ethan was startling.

'You look great, Lizzie. Tell me, how was Paris?'

'*Très* amazing, thank you. Just…amazing.' She turned to Leo, her eyes shining brightly. 'Can we tell them? Please?'

Her husband gave her an indulgent smile, his love evident in the protective arm round her shoulder and pride shimmering in his face as he looked only at her but spoke to the room. 'Okay… so, we have news.'

'I'm pregnant!' Lizzie blurted out, running a hand over her still flat stomach. 'We're having a baby.'

Leo kissed the top of her head. 'Yes. And we couldn't be more happy.'

Some people could have it all—work, marriage, love. As flutters of sadness whirled through her gut Kara forced out a smile, feeling, she thought, exactly the way Ethan looked right now: empty. Hollowed out.

But still he stepped forward and again shook his brother's hand, almost as if he was doing what he knew was polite rather than what he deep down wanted to do. 'Congratulations.'

'That's great news!' Declan gave them all a broad grin. 'Really fantastic. Seems it's all weddings and babies at the moment. Do you think there's something in the water?'

'Oh, yes, it's Grace and Mitchell's wedding in a couple of weeks, isn't it? Exciting!' Lizzie positively glowed with happiness. She glanced at her watch. 'Gosh, look, we really should go. We haven't even made it home yet, but Leo wanted to pop in here just to let you know we're back. You know what he's like—this clinic is his baby and he couldn't possibly drive past and not say hi.'

'You mean he wanted to see if the place has managed to survive without him? I think we've coped. Just.' Declan laughed. 'But you must be tired after your travels. Take your wife home, man. You have another baby to think about now. You can play surgeon-in-chief tomorrow.'

'Okay. Okay. I'll be in first thing tomorrow, if you can spare the time for a hand-over?' Leo looked at both Declan and Ethan, who nodded in agreement.

'Of course.'

And with that bombshell Leo walked his new bride out, their excited chatter resonating off the walls as they wandered down the corridor. Ethan followed a moment later, muttering something about a case arriving from Afghanistan in an hour or so and how not everyone needed to wear their hearts on their sleeves. Leaving Kara alone again with Declan, a whirlwind of emotions fluttering through her stomach.

Grateful that it wasn't her own private life in the spotlight, she commented on the scene that had just played out. 'Was it just me or did Ethan not seem particularly thrilled at the prospect of becoming an uncle?'

'He's had a rough ride, Kara. You of all people should understand that.'

Yes, she knew enough about rough times. About loss and grief. About the way dreams didn't become reality. That no matter how hard you tried to love someone, sometimes it wasn't enough. 'I guess...'

'Having seen first-hand how traumatic injuries affect soldiers...'

'Oh, yes. Of course.'

Declan shrugged and walked her towards the door, his hand on the small of her back, its heat sending her mind into a fuzz.

'But I think it's more than that. Between you and me, I think Ethan might be a touch jealous of Leo's happiness. It's something he's not been able to find for himself.'

'I heard they don't have an easy relationship.'

'There were issues between them in the past… That's why he joined the army, apparently—to get away from the messed-up Hunter family dynamic. And that, in turn, is why he's like he is now.'

She thought back to the way Ethan's jaw had tightened at the pregnancy news, the shadows that had formed under his eyes, the hollows in his cheekbones—jealousy? Without a doubt.

But she also knew that you had to dig very deep and get through tough times—find another focus, like work, and bury yourself in it. There was no point dwelling on what you couldn't change. It seemed Ethan, with his devotion to his work, was following the same mantra.

'Hey, are you okay?' Declan touched her arm. 'You seem a little quiet.'

If he'd just move his hand she wouldn't feel like leaning against him. Confiding in him. Asking him to kiss her again, fourth time lucky.

'Is that so strange?'

'Actually, yes. I never thought… All this talk of weddings must hit a raw nerve for you.'

The wedding hadn't been the problem. It had been the marriage. 'My wedding was a long time ago…it was a perfect day, exactly how I'd planned it. It's just a shame everything turned out the way it did in the end. But I'd never begrudge anyone a bit of happiness.'

'Fair play to you, Kara. That's my girl.'

His voice softened as his hand ran up her spine in a tender gesture that made her want to rest her head on those broad shoulders and just stop. Stop fighting this attraction. Stop trying to do the right thing when she wanted so desperately to do the wrong thing—with him.

'And you're staying on the team? No more talk of leaving?'

She pulled herself away from him. She'd managed perfectly well on her own up to now and she could do it again. And again. Unlike his mother and Safia she didn't need Declan's strength. She had enough of her own. She knew not to rely on anyone else because when it came down to it their promises pretty well amounted to nothing. Especially men like Declan—players; men who wanted everything but gave little in return. Well, he could have her one hundred per cent work commitment and that was all.

'I guess you boxed me into a corner there. So, yes, I suppose I'll stay. Even though now Leo's back you won't be so busy.'

'I'm always busy. I like it that way. Besides, he'll need time to catch up.' He gave her a wicked smile that threw her a challenge. 'Think you can keep your hands off me?'

'Oh, don't worry, Declan. I *know* I can.' Even though it would take a huge effort. 'Good night.'

Then she walked out of his office without looking back. Truth was, she had no idea how she was going to get through the next few weeks with any scrap of sanity left.

CHAPTER SEVEN

ALL WENT WELL for the next two weeks. Kara managed to maintain a respectable distance and Declan appeared to be trying too. Not once had they shared another kiss, or even a proximity that might generate one, even in the moments they spent together going over their cases.

Although the heat flickered between them like a smouldering fire—one small, wayward spark and she had no doubt things could get way out of control—she kept a lid on her emotions during the day. Only at night did she allow herself to relive those moments of closeness she'd shared with him.

So it was good to get some perspective now, on a rare day off, on her own out in the fresh air, taking in some of London's famous sights.

Having taken way too many photographs of the magnificent Globe Theatre, she wandered along Queen's Walk by the Thames. Barges glided past, and a cruise tour boat with people hanging out of open windows, cameras snapping, pointing and laughing. The river was as busy as the land on this bright sunny day.

In the distance the iconic sand-coloured Westminster Palace and its famous clock tower, Big Ben, dominated the view. She wandered along the paved walkway, weaving through the clusters of tourists taking photographs, past buskers and living statues, dodging jugglers and Latin American street dancers that added an exotic pulse to the atmosphere. The park was just a little farther along, next to the London Eye Ferris wheel, where somehow Mitchell and Grace had managed to land permission to hold their wedding reception.

Seemed most people from the Hunter Clinic had wrangled a day off to join in the festivities. Thank goodness she hadn't followed through on her request to transfer; she would have missed being here with this group of people who had invited her into their sophisticated yet welcoming world.

Some of her colleagues stood in the corner,

laughing, chatting. Kara began to approach, but just at that moment she saw Declan join them.

Heart thudding against her ribcage, she turned away.

With a toned body like his, encased in a dove-grey collared shirt and smart black trousers, he was bordering on illegally sexy.

Oh, please bring back the scrubs.

So much for perspective. How the heck could she get an ounce of that when he was within touching distance?

Keeping her back turned to Declan, she waved at the beaming bride and groom and at Mitchell's adorable daughter, Mia, who was the absolute darling of the piece. And, no, not once did she feel a pang of nostalgia for her own wedding—although she did fight back the sting of tears at the smiling faces, the sweet beauty of the love-conquers-all message.

Because she knew, deep in her heart of hearts, that sometimes love just wasn't enough to keep two people together. Which was so *not* how she should be feeling at a wedding.

She plastered a smile to her face, which wasn't too difficult because Grace and Mitchell's love shone through. 'Congratulations! Happy day! You look gorgeous!'

Voices behind her grew louder. One of them was Declan's. Her back stiffened.

'Oh…er…I'll be off now,' she heard him say. 'Got to go.'

'Wait,' the other male voice said.

Was it Ethan? Leo? She didn't dare turn to take a look.

'Is that Kara on her own? Come and say hi.'

God, no. Her heart dropped.

Declan's voice grew louder. 'No, seriously, I should go. I've got things to sort out.'

So he didn't want to face her either. And why did that not please her as much as it should?

The not-as-smooth-as-Declan's voice shouted, 'Kara! Hey!'

All well and good to avoid proximity in the busyness of work. But out here, in the sunshine, when she'd been caught alone, they were destined to at least talk. Anything less would appear rude.

Drawing a deep breath, she turned. Declan was standing in front of her on his own now, eyes blazing with frustration, his friend having disappeared into a huddle of suited men shaking hands and laughing.

He shrugged and raised his beer bottle. 'Hi.'

'Hi.'

'Nice day for a wedding,' he said politely, picking his words carefully.

The tiny hairs on her arms prickled at the voice. Warm and thick like Irish whiskey, it soothed her to the pit of her stomach. But also, like the strong dark liquor, it made her giddy and excitable.

'Yes.' She drew a breath and steadied her nerves. 'I thought I'd come along and take a sticky beak.'

His smile was breathtaking. 'There you go with that foreign language again. A what?'

'A look. A nosy. My flatmates have gone away for a few days so I was at a loose end. I just took a stroll along the riverfront. I never knew there was so much along here.'

He glanced down at her wedge sandals—honestly, they were only a few inches high…

'Really? Strolling in *those*?'

'Yes, Declan, what else would you do in them?' She held up her hand at the glint in his eye. *Do not take them off.* Suddenly her imagination ran riot with images of him naked…her legs wrappe around his. Heat seeped through her. 'Do not answer that.'

'Don't worry, we're in a public place—I do know how to behave.'

His voice lowered into a growl that simultaneously made her laugh and stoked something hot and needy in her stomach.

'I've been behaving for the past two damned weeks.'

So he was suffering too. That gave her a short blast of something wild and exciting. To have a man have to control himself around her gave her a sense of strength—power too. Something she hadn't had for a while.

'And so you shall continue.' She looked up into his dark brown eyes and thought that out here in broad daylight she was very unlikely to kiss him. Especially when they would be surrounded by people from the clinic. Despite how much she was drawn to that mouth. 'We're going to stick to safe subjects…like work.'

'Really?' His shoulders slumped forward. 'Dull.'

'Safe.'

'Dull.'

'Shut up. Actually, I was wanting to talk to you about Safia while we have a few minutes. I'm still worried about her.'

Kara had been meaning to catch up with him about the Princess for a couple of days, but an emergency case had taken priority.

He became serious in an instant. 'Me too. She's healing well, but my pep talk didn't really help.'

'Oh, it did. It was exactly what she needed to hear.'

And it had certainly helped Kara get more insight into the workings of his mind. Flirty and funny he might be, but he held people at an emotional distance, carrying baggage almost as big as hers, along with a huge responsibility for a family he tried hard not to care for.

'She's definitely more motivated, but she's still very down. Her parents got her tickets for the Oblivion concert and she didn't even show a flicker of interest.'

'When a girl stops showing interest in a sex god there is something very wrong.' He smirked and held his arms out, puffing his chest and smoothing his fingers through his hair. 'I should know.'

He was a sex god?

Spasms of lust rippled through her as he laughed. Yes. He was a sex god.

He was driving her crazy with his easy nonchalance, his wicked humour, his sexy talk. Crazy and just a little bit sexually frustrated. She took a bottle of water from her handbag and had a long, refreshing drink, hoping the cold might wash some sense into her. It didn't.

His eyes followed the movement in her throat as she swallowed. His gaze was bordering on insatiable. 'You are way too cocky, mate.'

'You just don't know what you're missing.'

Oh, but she did. Knew it with every single second she spent with him. Knew too that keeping a distance was definitely the only path to take.

She tried to relax and move the conversation to less shaky or sexy ground. 'Funny how life works out. I never thought I'd be working in London, walking alongside the Thames on a day off, visiting places where Shakespeare had been.'

'You had a different life planned?'

'Yes.' Rob was supposed to have left the army. They were supposed to have had a family, settled down. Found somewhere to belong, to fit. 'But ere I am, a long way from that.' Making her new life fit around her instead.

He walked her slowly to a patch of grass. Laying his jacket out, he indicated for her to sit. 'Your poor feet need a break. I have about five minutes, then I really do have to go.'

Good, setting out parameters.

Glancing around, she saw that most people had sat down in little huddles, or couples, spreading out in the park. Everyone seemed relaxed, paired off, settled in the sun. To interrupt them by barging into their groups would seem rude. Not to sit down for five minutes would too.

She determined to stay just long enough to be polite. 'What about you, Declan? Did you always want to come here? Where is it you're from again?'

'County Dublin.'

'Do you miss it?'

'Not really. I miss the fresh air, mostly, but you can't beat London for excitement. I love it here. No pressures. I like to be free. No ties.'

No ties. Like her. And yet whereas he clearly wanted to cast his ties off, she'd spent a good deal of time over the years trying to forge them one way or another. It was just that she'd tied hers to the wrong people.

'I've always wanted to visit Ireland—it sounds wonderful. I think somewhere back in our family's past we have people from there.'

'Most folks do.'

His hand brushed against hers and it would have been so easy to grasp it. But instead she shoved her fist in her dress pocket and let herself be carried away by his voice.

'It's a grand place to bring up kids. I can see that now, living in a big city like London where there's noise and pollution and crime, but I couldn't wait to escape. There were times I didn't think I'd ever leave the village I grew up in.'

Was this a good time to broach the subject? Unanswered questions swirled in her head and she felt compelled to know more and more about him. He seemed relaxed, just chatting.

Her heart thumped a little as she asked, 'Was that…because of the fire? Was she badly hurt… your mum?'

'She was close to not making it. Not just physically but emotionally.'

can't imagine how bad that was for you all. What about your dad? Was he hurt?'

His eyes clouded like dark storms. But it wasn't grief, it was anger. 'Not badly enough.'

Wow. Bitterness flowed from him. 'What do you mean? What happened?'

'That's a lot of questions, Kara.' He put his hand on her shoulder. 'I prefer to look ahead now, eh? No point in dwelling on all that.'

She looked up into those clouds, saw fear there too, and hurt. She wanted to wrap him in her arms and wipe away that pain. But he would never let her do that—he was too proud, too closed-off.

'You mean, back right off.'

'Yes, I do. Leave it alone.'

At least this time his tone was gentle—but she'd overstepped the mark. In lots of ways he was right. There was no point dwelling on the past, even if it did tinge everything you felt— your dreams, your plans. Taking a long deep breath, she looked ahead.

Adults laughed and chatted, children of all ages played together, teenagers swung toddlers around, made daisy chains, chatted happily alongside each other.

With a sorry heart she thought about Safia in her hospital room, so far away from her friends and surrounded by stuffy aides and parents who desperately wanted to make her feel better but were at a loss as to what to do.

But as she watched a thought crystallised.

Declan lay back on his elbow and gave her a lazy smile. His hair kind of flopped over his eyes just a little, and once again she found herself fighting the urge to run her fingers through it. The clouds in his eyes had passed through and she saw only light in them now.

'I have an idea.'

'Oh?' His eyebrows peaked. 'Should I be worried? Scared? Excited?'

'All of the above.' She winked. 'Brace yourself.'

Declan sat up as Kara smoothed her pale yellow linen dress around her. He'd thought he'd been doing quite well, sticking to safe conversations and being on his best behaviour. And, truth be told, he'd spent two whole weeks reining in his libido to the point of utter frustration—and, man, he'd been good. In Theatre, on the ward rounds, in meetings, he'd maintained a professional distance, had kept his dirty mouth in check, had not touched her. Not once.

And while once upon a time if his libido had been bouncing like this he'd have gone out and got laid with a like-minded woman, recently he just hadn't had the appetite. But now the sight of those long tanned legs and cute *kiss me* mouth made his heart jump more than a little.

'So...' She gifted him a smile, which turned the heart-flip into a full-scale bungee. 'Now that she's had her second lot of surgery do you think Safia is well enough to be in a shared room?'

'Work, work, work. Of course.' He tipped his head back and laughed.

The woman was either work-obsessed or choosing her conversation topics with absolute care. Judging by the pink tinge to her cheeks, and the resolute way she would not look him fully in the eye, he guessed it was a bit of both.

'Yes, she's healing well, but her parents have specifically requested for her to be on her own. They are very strict on privacy.'

'Yes, I understand that. She might be a princess, but really, as you say, she's just like a other girl. She wants to be with friends, to cha and laugh and squeal over boys. I think she's lonely, and I think she needs normal.'

'And moving her to a shared room would give her company, distract her from her burns. Genius.'

It was a simple idea, but often they were the best ones. He'd been so focused on keeping the girl safe and her parents happy that he'd skipped past Safia's basic needs. Companionship.

Hell, the more he thought about it the more he could apply that logic to himself. But he'd never wanted companionship before—at least not past the bedroom door—so God knew why suddenly he felt as if he'd been missing something...he didn't want to think about what.

'What about the cross-infection risk?'

Kara leaned forward and he caught a flash of pure white lace under the halterneck dress. His mind whizzed into overdrive. The trouble with halternecks was the sheer amount of skin exposed. Her neckline, sun-kissed shoulders, a wide expanse of back that made him want to stroke his fingers down that spine.

But the best bit about halternecks was the mount of skin exposed…the neckline, sun-kissed shoulders…

Yes, he knew exactly what he'd been missing. And looking at those long limbs, that easy smile, the curve of her breasts, he could only guess what else he was missing too.

As if he'd ever dreamt that a loudmouthed Aussie might fill a gap in his life that he didn't even know he had. Confused wasn't the half of it.

He dragged his eyes away and reminded himself of their conversation. *Cross-infection risk.* 'Minimal, I'd say. At least at the moment while she's still on prophylactic antibiotics. She should be fine. We'd just need to keep an eye on her temp and wound sites. I'll talk to her parents and run it by them. I'm not sure they'll be very happy at the prospect of moving her.'

'But we're talking about her mental health here, not just physical. Surely they'll see that?'

'I'll discuss it with them. That's all I can promise.'

His cell phone rang. *Damn.* Not today.

Her eyes flicked to his phone, lying on the

grass next to him, but truly he didn't even need to check to see who was calling.

'Aren't you going to answer it?'

'Nah. It's just family stuff.' He'd deal with it later. He took a long slug of his beer. *Later.*

'Then surely you should pick up?'

'Look, I'm having a good time.' The ringing stopped. 'See. She'll leave a message.'

It rang again.

Kara's gaze hooked on to his. 'It might be important.'

'It's Niamh. It won't be.'

Kara's eyes narrowed with suspicion. 'How do you know? How do you even know it's Niamh?'

'She has a special ringtone so I know when to answer. Or rather, when not to answer.' He laughed. 'You know, they're great, but, man, *so* needy. I'm at a friend's wedding, for goodness' sake. This…' He indicated the setting, the weather, his beer. *Her.* 'This is nice.'

Days off were scarce; spending them outdoors with a beautiful woman were rare indeed.

His phone rang again.

'It's okay. Pick up. Seriously, I don't mind.' She reached for the phone and glared at him. But her smile was sweet and she was laughing. 'Declan, come on, it might be important. What if it was and you missed something? Family's important. Just be grateful you have one that cares.'

He saw the flicker of hurt as she flapped a hand in front of her and shook her head. *Don't go there.* But he remembered the bitter words she'd used back in that corridor weeks ago. *What their child wanted came at the bottom of the pecking order.*

She'd clearly had a bad run, with parents who cared more for their careers than for her needs. And her husband had left her a widow so young.

Hell, his family might irritate him but he knew he was loved—even if it was to the point that it felt suffocating.

'Okay. Okay. But I know I'm going to regret this.'

He huffed out a breath and snatched her hand away, grabbing her fingers and holding them. She playfully pulled back, but she didn't wriggle from his grip. Her skin was warm on his. Every single nerve-ending fired into action.

And there…right there…that second…the electricity between them sparked into life again.

Need slammed into him. She felt it too, he knew
He could just see the playful teasing in her eyes
melt into something dangerous and hot. Her smile
wavered into the bite of her teeth on her bottom
lip, the reddening of her skin, the quickening of
her breath.

She didn't want this. But she did. And, *God*,
he wanted her like nothing and no one he'd
ever wanted before. He'd held back and held
back…

He caught her chin with his hand and tilted her
head to his. Her mouth was only inches away.
Her tongue darted out and wet her lips as if she
was about to eat something delicious.

Kiss me.

And he was going to. As he lowered his mouth
towards hers the earth twisted on an axis he
couldn't fathom and the breath was stripped from
his lungs. And, sure, his whole damned work-
place was here, watching again. Like before—
that first time on the ballroom floor.

And just like that first time he couldn't stop
himself—couldn't stop the pull of her lips, of her
fragrance. He just wanted her in his arms. There

was a connection—not just a base physical attraction, something more—that drew him to her.

He was going to kiss her once more, just to get her well and truly out of his system. Then he was going to put a stop to these flirting shenanigans and focus on his life and responsibilities.

'Declan?'

She fitted so perfectly into his arms. Her breath was on his throat like a butterfly kiss. Her voice was hoarse, and he definitely caught the sexy catch.

'Aren't you going to answer it, then?'

The phone. The damned phone.

He exhaled and kept his voice steady—this time not from frustration but from pure, blatant, feral need. Clearly his sister didn't need to hear that.

'Niamh. This had better be important.'

'Hello to you too, Dec. Now, I was just planning ahead awhile… You know Mammy's birthday's coming up…'

Please. Really? Mid-pash? 'Can this not wait?'

'Why? What the hell are you up to on a fine Saturday afternoon?'

He growled. 'You don't want to know.'

'Wrong, Declan. I *do* want to know. What's her name?'

Was nothing private? 'None of your business.'

'Sure, that's an odd name for a girl. Now, tear yourself away and talk to me about Mammy's birthday. She'd love to see you here…'

He listened to his sister blather on and his blood pressure started its usual upward hike as his libido crashed into his boots. 'I'll see what I can do, but you know what it's like. I do have work to do.' He dragged his hand away from Kara, stood and took a few paces away so she wouldn't hear the drama. 'We're fierce short-staffed as it is.'

'It's always work with you, Dec. But I think seeing you would be a real tonic for her.'

'I have to work, for God's sake.' What more did they want from him? He sent home a good amount of money, and it was a far cry from what he'd been forced to do as a kid just to get some food on the table. At least he was on the right side of the law now. 'How the hell else do we pay for the things you all want? Look, I'll see what I can do.'

In reality, he didn't want to face the endless questions that Niamh seemed to think were per-

fectly acceptable for a girl to ask her brother…
and added to five-fold by the rest of his siblings
and his mother.

When are you settling down?

What about babies?

Found a nice girl yet?

Despite her own experiences his mother seemed
to think that the answer to life, the universe
and everything was finding a nice girl. He'd
found plenty. He just hadn't loved any of them.
And didn't plan to any time this side of the millennia.

'Look, I'll get back to you. I have things to do.'

'Okay, big brother, think about it. Be good.
And be careful. And if you can't be careful…
you know the drill. Buy a pram.'

Yada. Yada.

He flicked the phone into his pocket and inhaled deeply, trying to find the equilibrium that
had been shattered first by a sexy siren and then
by his stroppy sister.

Once calm, he turned back, ready to start again
with Kara. 'Now, where were we…?'

But she'd disappeared.

He searched the crowd and saw her walking back to the main wedding group, being led by a pair of too-cute little girls in party dresses that reminded him of happier days with his sisters— before the fire had maimed their mother, sent their feckless father running away from his responsibilities and catapulted Declan into being the main breadwinner when there were no jobs for a scrawny kid, no way of earning money to pay for things.

And still, so many years later, they relied on him for everything.

As if she could sense his eyes on her smooth, straight back, Kara turned and scanned for him. Once she'd found him she shrugged a little, her eyes bright but her smile regretful. Regretful about what? he wondered. That things had nearly got out of control again? Or regretful that they hadn't?

And then, as she wandered through the wedding party, he thought perhaps Kara's feelings were all mixed up with her own past. Did she regret coming to a wedding that would surely bring back memories of her own and of her war hero husband? Was that why he'd felt her tiny

...ift towards temptation? Did she just need comfort?

And why the hell did he care? Because the last thing he needed was another woman to worry about.

CHAPTER EIGHT

'SAFIA IS PROGRESSING very well indeed, at least physically.'

True to his word, Declan was presenting Kara's idea to Safia's parents in the burns unit family meeting room. Their first meeting since the weekend was going well so far.

No, their first meeting with *Safia's parents* was going well…but Kara was struggling with the near-kiss thing, and how easily she fell under Declan's spell every darned time. A lucky save by that pair of darling girls had put an end to something before it had started, but she was losing self-control with every touch, every look, every minute she spent with him.

Especially when he was dressed, like today, in a smart dark suit and an open-necked camel-coloured shirt. One tiny glimpse of his chest and she was a quivering mess of hormones. And it was way too early in the day for that.

'We have completed phases one to three of her management so far. She is alive and thriving, her burns are now all in a closed healing phase. She is having regular therapy to prevent contractures and she is responding well to that.'

The Sheikh nodded. 'Yes, we are delighted with your care. We are most grateful. She is getting better.'

'Well, yes. Her wounds are healing.' Declan leaned forward and frowned. He seemed to be choosing his approach carefully. 'But I'm concerned about her low mood.'

'She is sad, but she'll feel better soon.' Safia's mother had clucked around her daughter like an anxious mother hen from the minute they'd arrived. And who wouldn't? Who wouldn't fight for their child's life? Love for her daughter shone through, but it was a little…stifling.

'Until a few years ago burns specialists spent a lot of time and emphasis just on treating the burns and keeping the patient alive. Now survival is much more likely that we have to look at how patients like Safia are going to fare in the future, once they've been released from hospital. That's why we've been giving her physiotherapy since the day she arrived.'

'But I don't know what to do with her. She just sits and stares out of the window.'

Declan nodded, his hands clasped in front of him, his eyes soft and gentle. 'I know. I know. And I understand how upsetting it is for you to see her like this. We need to get her interested in things again. What does she like doing?'

'Make-up, clothes, horse-riding. She…you know…*hangs out*. In our country obviously she studies, goes to parties…shopping…friends. But she won't let them come to see her. We'd fly them in, but she refuses to see anyone.' The Sheikha nervously toyed with the edge of her beaded shawl. 'She's always got an opinion on everything. She's a handful at times. But now she doesn't seem interested in anything.'

'Ms Stephens has an idea we want to run by you.'

Declan's eyes fell on Kara, making her pulse jump in a skittering dance. *Damn. Stop it, already.*

'We thought, perhaps, that Safia might ben-fit from sharing a room with other people her own age?'

'Absolutely not.' Sheikh El-Zayad's voice filled the room. He was a man used to getting his own way, who commanded everyone and everything. 'I appreciate your concern, Mr Underwood, and I'm very grateful for your help in her progress, but my daughter shares a room with no one. She is the Sheikha of Aljahar—a princess. She does not mix with other...ordinary people. We have paid for privacy—it is very important to us.'

Declan shot a quick look over to Kara. No one else would have noticed but his jaw had tightened just a little. He took a deep breath and smiled, his voice now soothing, but with an authoritative edge.

'We could compromise. Perhaps she doesn't necessarily need to share a room—but she does need stimulation. It's very important she has contact with people her own age—not just your aides and...yourselves. The physiotherapist is happy to come and attend to her in her room—but I do think she needs to be occupied for the other hours of the day. At the very least she should come out and join in some activities, eat her meals with the others. Long-term psychological effects people with burns injuries are well documente We need to keep her motivated.'

Kara knew he wasn't just talking about his professional experience. So his actions and his words were oceans apart. Because, yes, even though she'd tried hard not to listen in to his private conversation with his sister she'd caught snippets.

He was refusing to go and visit them—and using work as an excuse. Maybe it was easier dealing with someone who wasn't a relative than having to face your own realities at home.

'With all due respect, Your Highnesses...' She smiled to them both, knowing her voice was rising just a little. 'Integration is a huge part of our therapy here. I don't want to alarm you, but I know you appreciate honest talking...' She waited until she'd received a positive response from them. 'Safia won't get better unless she sees some normality in her life—she's had enough of pain and being shut in that room on her own. I'm concerned about the risk of depression. She needs to be engaged. And she needs, really, to be part of this discussion.'

'Thank you, Kara.'

afia's voice had them all turning quickly to
e her standing in the hallway. Dressed in jeans
and a baggy sweatshirt, she looked like a regular teenager apart from the left side of her face
and her hands which were covered in dressings.

She was pale and unsmiling. 'Talking about
me again, Daddy?'

Declan stood and brought Safia into the room,
offered her a seat. 'Hey. Thanks for coming by.
It's nice to see you out of that room for a change.
It must be boring on your own all day?'

'*Duh*. Of course.' Safia shook her head, her
black curls bobbing round her shoulders.

As a member of a famous royal family her photos had graced the newspapers from an early age;
her face was well known. She'd been a pretty
girl—a beautiful teenager. Kara's heart clenched
at what the future held for Safia now. She couldn't
begin to imagine the grief and loss the girl felt.

She watched as Declan and Safia sat across
from each other, saw his generous smile and a
concern that went beyond his professional ob-
ligation. He pointed through the glass door to
the ward where, as luck would have it, a seven-
teen-year-old boy who'd been brought in after a

freak lightning strike had burnt his back, walked past. Wearing teen trademark baggy-bottomed trousers that hung off his hips, and a sideswiped fringe, he stopped and gave Safia a hesitant smile. Then a sort of half-wave before he disappeared into the ward.

Declan watched this with interest, a hint of a smile playing over his lips. 'But I bet you wouldn't be interested in spending time out there, Safia? Although Jack's got an interesting story to tell.'

The girl shrugged, but there was a spark in her eyes. Finally they'd got her interested in something. 'Anything's got to be better than sitting around with you lot.'

Declan grinned. 'Feeling better already?'

'Maybe.'

Kara glanced to Safia's parents, who looked at each other and shook their heads. They murmured quietly in a language Kara didn't understand and finally Safia's mother sighed. 'Okay. If you think so. Do it.'

'Wait—' Sheikh El-Zayad tried to speak, but his wife stopped him, patting him on the knee.

She turned to Declan and winked, 'Don't worry. Leave him to me.'

It was very early days but Kara took the wins as they came. Safia needed to be stimulated and motivated—whatever it took. 'Okay, as soon as there's a bed free we'll move her in. Until that happens, how about we take a little stroll down through the main ward and see who's hanging out?'

Please be there, lightning boy.

'Yes.' Declan nodded his thanks to the Sheikh and Sheikha and bowed them through the door first, then followed with Safia. 'There's a games console over there. You fancy your chances against me?'

The Princess frowned. 'A video game?'

'Why not? It's great therapy for those thumbs.'

'Daddy would have a fit.'

She gave them her first real smile for weeks. But then surely anyone would have to smile with the offer of a few more minutes in Declan's company?

'You're on.'

It was late when Kara eventually managed to snatch time to write up her case notes for the day. Hiding out in Declan's offices at Kate's,

she'd dodged the Sheikh's aides with their end
less questions about maintaining Safia's dignity
in the face of such intrusions as sharing the patients' TV room. Funny, what most people took
for granted they'd had to fight for, for Safia—just
some friends, a little hope…

Kara's feet ached—but then that was nothing
new. Her head ached—but that was becoming a
habit whenever Declan was around. Too much
arousal could do that to a girl. The sooner she was
home and out of the Declan Underwood temptation zone the better. Gathering her paperwork together and stuffing it in her bag she finished up.

The phone rang. *Damn.* She looked round for
someone to answer it, but of course his secretary
had left for the day, and Declan was consulting
next door. Who the hell would ring his rooms
so late?

Sighing, she picked up. 'Mr Underwood's phone.'

'Can I speak to Declan, please?' The voice
was soft and sweet, unmistakably Irish. Niamh?
Aoife? Briana? Roisin?

'I'm afraid he's consulting at the moment. Can
I take a message?'

There was a frustrated sigh. 'Sure. But it won't

ake a blind bit of notice. Tell him Niamh rang and he must call me back...*immediately*. It's very important.'

'You could try his mobile phone?'

'It's rung and rung to the voice mail a million times. The man's either got cloth ears or he's avoiding me. I'm resorting to underhand tactics and phoning him at work.' There was a smile in her voice. 'He hates that.'

The smile was catching, Declan's sister seemed warm and friendly—the kind of sister Kara would have liked if she'd been lucky enough to have one. 'Don't worry, I'll tell him. Oh, wait—he's just here.'

He'd come through the adjoining door.

'Still here? It's after five...'

He grinned and her heart melted. His eyes glittered, and the soft upward curve of his lips was like a promise.

'You know what that means.'

The five o'clock rule. Kissing was apparently allowed, according to him. Not her.

Dragging her heart back behind its steel barrier, she pointed to the receiver in her hand. 'Niamh's on the phone. She says it's important.'

'It's always important.' He threw some file onto his secretary's desk and shook his head. 'Tell her I'll call her later.'

Kara grinned. 'He's just coming, Niamh. He's—'

'Hey, I can wait all night. Just don't, for God's sake, try making excuses for him. He's a terrible liar. Tell him I've got more willpower than he'll ever have and I can keep ringing until he answers. And I will.'

Kara had no doubt that Niamh was just as willful as Declan.

They clearly all loved each other in a very definite sibling kind of way. Kara covered the speaker and held it out to Declan, shaking her head. 'She said she's had to resort to underhand tactics...'

She looked at the tired lines around his eyes, the tight clench of his jaw. Here he was, at way too late o'clock, still at work, planning his Theatre list for tomorrow, seeing clients after hours to make sure he could fit them into his schedule, attending to the needs of everyone but himself. And now this.

With a shock she realised how much she wanted

see him smile again. To feel the warmth of his smile on her, his breath, his touch. And soon.

'Do you always inspire such devious strategies in women?'

'Sadly only the ones I'm trying to avoid.' Glancing at the phone he let his eyebrows dip into a frown. Then he looked back at her.

She saw the mirrored need in his eyes—a raw need that fired something deep in her, something that shivered through each nerve-ending. Heat pooled in her gut, and lower, and then he was next to her, one hand in her hair, the other on her back. His mouth was on her neck.

'Declan.' She thrust the phone towards him. 'Your family loves you enough to be bothered. Talk to your sister. Be nice. That is all.'

'What is this? Secrets of the sour, sassy sisterhood?' He let out a contrite sigh. 'Ah, hell, give it here.'

Damn. Declan grabbed the phone, once again torn between the woman in front of him and his family's needs. He'd been too close to grabbing her and having her against that wall. To losing himself in her.

'Niamh. This had damn well better be important.'

'Hello to you too, Declan.' His sister lowered her voice. 'So, are you sleeping with her yet?'

'What?' His eyes popped as he strode across the room, out of Kara's earshot. 'No.'

'But you want to—she sounds nice. Won't take any crap from you, I wouldn't think.'

'Niamh, what do you want?'

'Apart from a big brother who shows his face every now and then? Sure, Declan, I can't remember what your ugly features look like these days.' She sighed. 'Is she pretty?'

He glanced at Kara, who now appeared to be nose-deep in a patient's notes. He looked at the soft golden shine on her hair, the way her lips twitched, that mouth that tasted of sunshine and sweetness.

'Yes. Very. Now, this is exactly why I live in London—to get away from all this…interrogation.'

'No, you live in London to get away from all those poor broken-hearted Dublin girls who wanted to make a decent man of you… And to avoid the truth.'

The truth that he would never be a decent man, because every time a woman had made those happy-ever-after kind of ministrations he'd run a mile. A sea. A country.

'Niamh. Leave it.'

'Will you come over for Mammy's birthday? Please? She won't be happy until she sees you again.'

'She won't be happy until I'm married off to the lowest bidder.' His heart squeezed. Poor Mammy…all she'd ever wanted was for him to be happy—but in her book that meant marriage.

He wasn't convinced. He'd seen the destruction marriage, and the end of it, had wreaked on *her*.

'I'll send her something. I can't—' Couldn't face going back. Couldn't look at her and know he'd failed her—in every way. He hadn't saved her from being hurt, and now he couldn't give her what she wanted most—hope. 'Yep. I'll send her something.'

'She doesn't need your flowers. She needs to see you. It's her sixtieth and she needs something to celebrate. When did you last come home? Can you even remember?'

No. Shame hit him in the gut. Working in London meant he could earn more cash than he ever would back home—which in turn meant he could support his family and have a life.

'I don't know—I can't face all those questions...' He turned his back and whispered, 'She's forever on my back.'

Niamh laughed. 'She just wants to know you're happy all the way over there. A bunch of flowers doesn't tell her that. Why don't you bring someone? That'd shut Mammy up. Hey, what about that girl? The one who answered the phone—?'

'Who? Kara?'

As he spoke Kara's head popped up. 'Yes?'

'Oh, sorry. Not you...' He pointed to the phone. 'It was...it's my sister.'

Niamh laughed again. 'Tongue-tied? You? Wow, you have it bad, big brother. Go on—ask her to come.'

Kara's eyes narrowed. She stood and picked up her handbag. 'What's she saying?'

Don't leave. Stuck in between two determined women, that was all he needed. But he wouldn't be taking her anywhere near his home.

'That...that the weather in Ireland's very warm...'

Kara waited, her eyes blinking innocently. 'The weather? Why—?'

'Coward!' Niamh hollered. 'Ask her. It'll get Mammy off your back.'

'Hmm...' He supposed his sister could be right. Having Kara there would be a delicious distraction. He could mix family with...a little pleasure. Would she? Could it work? How would it work? Hell, he didn't know, but it was a heck of a plan. Kara in his house... A man could think of worse ways to spend a couple of days.

Maybe it was time to go home.

He huffed out an exasperated breath. 'Niamh wants you to come visit Ireland.'

Kara stared, her hand on one hip. 'Your sister wants me to go to Ireland?'

'Just for a weekend. My mum's birthday. Sure, why not? You said you'd always wanted to visit the place.'

'No way.' Her hands were physically up in front of her. She didn't want this. She really didn't want this.

Niamh's voice crackled down the phone. 'Did she say yes?'

'Niamh, for heaven's sake leave us alone for a minute. She's thinking about it.'

Kara's cheeks reddened. 'Do you Underwoods always work in packs?'

'Believe me, my sisters could teach the army a thing or two about stealth operations.' But the more he thought about it, the more it became a perfect plan. '*They* want me to go back for her birthday. They said you should come too. *You* said I should be nice to my family. Bingo— everyone's happy. Say yes?'

'Emotional blackmail doesn't wear well on you, Declan.' She fiddled with her necklace.

'No ties, no strings.' At her frown he thought he'd better just be honest. 'Look, I just want to give Mammy some hope—to think that I'm off her hands. I...we...need her to stop worrying about us all and focus on her own life. There'll be the hassle of my sisters...but they're not so bad really.'

'No.'

But she'd released her grip on her bag. Was looking down at her magnificent shoes, out of the window, at the floor. She was wavering, he could tell.

Time to strike.

'I've tried my whole life to make her better—
and the only thing she's ever said she needed
was to see me settled and happy. She would love
you, Kara. It's just a weekend. Two nights. Two.
Nights.'

He held his fingers up just the way she had with
her *Two kisses* quip. He saw the flash of recognition and the rush of desire on her face—not just
in her eyes, but in the flush of her cheeks. And,
goddamn it, in the ghost of a sexy smile.

He imagined what he could do to her—with
her—in two nights. Hell, he'd settle for just two
hours. Naked. Shoes optional. Actually, shoes
definitely on.

'It's gorgeous at this time of year. The leaves
turning golden, the rolling hills. Ireland…land
of your ancestors.'

Then for a fleeting second he realised what a
stupid plan it was. Because above the pretence
and the joking he knew that he was actually falling for her. That some part of him wanted Kara
in his chaotic life—and that was the maddest
thing he'd ever thought. He wanted ties and that
made him scared as hell.

Because after the weekend he couldn't offer her anything apart from a return to this—late-night meetings in his office, early mornings in surgery and the craziness of hospital life in between. Just colleagues. And then she'd be gone anyway, back to her team, and he'd be left with catching the scent of her in corridors, fleeting glimpses across the cafeteria...

His voice wavered a little as the reality of the plan sank in. 'But if—'

She smiled. 'Oh, okay, what the hell? Why not? I'm going to regret this, I know, but when you describe it like that how can I refuse?'

CHAPTER NINE

KARA STARED OUT of the hire car window as the Dublin countryside flew past. Pink clouds melted into rolling hills, ten shades of green, as the sun began to set around them. It was nothing...*nothing* like the endless red dry earth of her childhood, the heat, the bright, cloudless blue skies.

Here, lush fields carved by stone walls as ancient as the earth itself spilled out in front of them to the left and right as far as she could see. Cows grazed lazily, and ignored their momentous arrival in Declan's home county.

Momentous? Sure. What kind of far-side-of-madness idea was this? Panic rolled through her in waves.

This weekend was going to be sheer torment— not least because she would have Declan within the temptation zone for forty-eight exhausting hours. But then, she couldn't deny she wasn't a teensy bit intrigued to see where he'd grown up and what had made him the complex man he was today. Even if the reason she was here was to cajole his mother into believing he was happy and settled.

She wondered if Declan was having second thoughts too as he stared ahead with eyebrows furrowed, his jaw fixed. His mood was hard to read—but he definitely wasn't in his happy-go-lucky, carefree place. The silence between them since they'd checked in at the airport had stretched and stretched, interspersed by brief words and *über*-politeness.

As he drove he glanced over to her and she must have looked either a fright, or frightened, because he managed a smile.

'Hey, don't look so worried. It'll be fine.'

It was more a question than a statement, and she wondered just who he was trying to convince.

'I know. I know. I'm just a little nervous about meeting everyone.'

'Ah, they'll love you. How could they not?'

'Okay.' She wanted to run her hand along his leg and pat it and smile, tell him she was okay and looking forward to it all—do the kind of things you'd do to a friend or a lover. But she couldn't because, really, she was neither.

And the frightening truth was, deep down, that she didn't want to live something over the weekend and later want it to be true. But it was already too late.

He pulled up outside a large farmhouse and she could see, in the dimming light, a number of smaller outer buildings dotting the acreage. With walls the colour of thick clotted cream, wide picture windows edged by pink roses, the house took her breath away. She imagined Declan as a child, running around, up to his neck in mud, playing and working on the farm.

He opened the car door for her and she stepped out into a surprisingly warm gentle breeze.

'Wow. It's so gorgeous. It's like a dream house. You grew up here?'

'Well, on the farm, yes.' His eyes darkened. 'But there was the fire, obviously…and so we built this.'

And there her images of him morphed from innocent to troubled. Her heart thudded. This place must bring back so many bleak memories for him. No wonder he barely wanted to visit.

'Ach, *Declan* built this.'

A thin, pretty woman with long dark hair stepped out through the front door, folded her flour-dusted arms and grinned.

'Not with his bare hands, you understand. Although he tried to in his weekends off from medical school. But he's a surgeon, not a builder—mighty fine with a knife, but we were deeply concerned about letting him loose with bricks and mortar. I'm Niamh. Pleased to meet you.' She stuck out her hand. 'Thank you for bringing him.'

'I...er...I didn't. He brought me, really. But nice to meet you too.' Kara shook Niamh's hand and immediately liked the warm, friendly welcome that put her a little more at ease.

'It was you on the phone, right?' At Kara's confusion Niamh explained, 'I recognise the accent. Australian? Kiwi?'

'Aussie.'

'I thought so. And I do get the feeling he wouldn't be here if you weren't. So you've done a grand job already.'

'Hello? I *can* hear you, you know.' Declan growled as he gave his sister's cheek a peck.

'Tosh, what do we care? And smile, Declan, it's only for a couple of days.' Niamh laughed. 'You certainly took your time getting here. And I don't mean the journey from the airport. Because that doesn't take a year and a half.'

Kara wondered what else Declan's sister thought behind those perceptive Underwood dark brown eyes. And, indeed, just what Declan had told her about the nature of her and Declan's relationship.

And then from behind Niamh came a roar, high-pitched squeals and a loud stamping along the wooden floor as four small children ran out and grabbed on to Declan's legs.

His face changed in an instant. His eyes lit up brightly and his smile stretched. 'Look at you all.' Swinging each one round in turn, he plastered a kiss on each plump cheek. 'Aine—pretty as a picture. Fiona—my, what a smile you've got. Saoirse—look at you.' Lastly he reached down between his legs and caught hold of a wee grinning boy. 'And Declan Junior—whoa, you've grown, my man. This is my friend, Kara. Say hi.'

'Hi, Kara,' they chorused, their curls bobbing

in time with their words, and Kara's heart just about melted.

'Hi, everyone. Very pleased to meet you…er… Aine, Fiona, Saoirse and Declan.' If she repeated the names she might have a hope of remembering them.

She bent to shake their chubby hands and before she knew it was almost bowled over by sticky fists and warm bodies pressing close in a sort of clumsy, grubby scrum.

'You talk funny,' Aine whispered.

'So do you.' Kara gave the girl a big smile and tapped the end of her cute snub nose with her finger. 'And you're gorgeous.'

'Well, come in, come in. The others won't be long.' Niamh ushered the children back into the house and was just turning round herself when she glanced down to Kara's feet. Her hand went to her chest. 'Oh, my…'

Kara followed Niamh's line of vision and lifted her foot up, all the better to see her beautiful red suede ankle boots with black ribbon ties. 'Oh, yes. These. Totally impractical, I know. But just for the journey…'

'I think I just fell in love with your girlfriend.

Clearly we're going to be great friends,' Niamh quipped to Declan as she led them into the house. 'You must tell me where you got them from.'

'Sure, I'd love to see you milking the cows in those,' Declan snapped, expertly avoiding the girlfriend comment.

But his eyes flickered towards Kara. She just couldn't read what he was thinking and once again she wondered what she was doing here—doing this.

'Come meet my mam.'

Kara's heart-rate trebled. Declan had explained that his mum was shy and very aware of her scarring, so it was important to put a lid on her loud-mouthed, out-there, army brat self.

But when Declan's hand fitted around hers and he walked her through the airy hallway to the large kitchen she stopped thinking and tried to just *be*. Which wasn't hard; being in his firm grip and the subject of his warm gaze made her lose track of her thought processes anyway.

The kitchen was everything Kara dreamt a family kitchen should be. Flour on the bench-top, creamy mounds of dough left to rise, a large wooden table covered in piles of pots and pans,

and a warm, herby cooking smell that made her nervous stomach grumble.

Once again she felt out of her depth. She'd never had a home like this—one that felt so welcoming, that smelt of flowers and yeast and clear fresh air, that was busy and chaotic and so full of life. A lump thickened her throat. It was everything she'd ever hoped for growing up, pretty much alone—the career, the husband, the home life. She'd believed she could have it all.

Until hard reality had smacked her in the gut and she'd been left with little more than broken dreams.

Mary Underwood sat in the corner of the room, looking out of the window across the blackening night. As they approached she looked up and inhaled sharply. Tugging down one side of her long grey bob to cover a good part of her face, she stood and offered Kara a shaky smile. 'Goodness, I can't believe you've come home with our Declan. You're awful pretty, Kara. Nice to meet you.'

Kara could see the muted sadness in those dark brown eyes. The same eyes every member of the family had. But all of them shimmered with something different. With Declan it was wickedness, or heat, or cool restraint. Niamh's were tired and yet somehow content, and held a little of the wicked in them. Mary's were filled with an almost tangible love for her son but edged with pain.

The cause was right there on the woman's face. Melted skin pulled down her features into nasty ridges like old candlewax. Her hands too were scarred and lined.

Kara stepped forward, unsure whether to kiss her or shake hands…or what to say. Words felt inadequate. 'Nice to meet you. Thank you for letting me come—especially for your birthday. I'm really happy to be here.'

'You and me both. I never thought I'd see the day.' Mary nodded, relaxing a little with each softly spoken word, but still tugging at her hair. 'Now, Declan, take Kara to the cottage and settle her in. Be sure to be back by seven for your dinner.'

'Aye, Mam, will do. It's good to see you.'

He wrapped his arms round his mother but she batted him away with a friendly smile. 'Away with you, now. Can't you see I'm busy?'

* * *

They walked through the encroaching darkness to a small house across a field. Declan opened the front door and ushered her in, shutting out the four sets of Underwood eyes that hung around in the paved area out front. Cute they might be, but clearly his nieces and nephew hadn't got the hang of adult time. And he needed a good shot of that right now.

Actually, he needed a good shot of London right now...with Kara as a chaser.

Yet here he was, for the first time in many months, with a *girlfriend* in tow. What a crazy, mixed-up idea that had been.

She peered up at him through thick black eyelashes, her green eyes piercing. 'Wow. This is so different to the main house. So...stark. And so not the twee cottage I had in mind.'

He plonked their bags down on the white-washed floorboards and looked round at the clean lines. No frills, no mess. Masculine. His. 'Home sweet home.'

'This is yours?'

'Yes. When I could, I made it my priority to have some space. Sharing with that amount of oestrogen is way too dangerous for my health. So when I come home this is my space. No unwanted interruptions...' He nodded to the giggling coming from the other side of the door. 'Not too many anyway. Ach, they'll get bored soon enough. You can have the main bedroom. I'm just next door. In case... Well, in case you need me. For anything.'

Declan put Kara's bag on the master bedroom floor.

'Oh? And just what would I need you for?'

'You may need help changing for dinner. I'm all yours for unzipping...unbuttoning...unclipping...' He leaned in closer, inhaled the scent of outdoors and coconut shampoo. 'I think you'll find I'm pretty adept at it.'

'I don't doubt that for a second, but I can manage.' Kara gave him a strange half-smile, her hand clutching the hem of her cashmere cardigan. He'd never seen her quite so unsettled.

He liked that. Liked that she was such a mixed bag of emotions, but that she was determined to deal with it herself—not demanding anything from him, not clingy. Nor did she ask about a future for them, or push him into a corner, or cause a drama. That was how he liked things—uncomplicated.

So why the hell he'd invited her here to make things very complicated he didn't know. But he reminded himself they had only two days to do this. Then they would be free to go back to their uncomplicated lives in London.

Only now London didn't seem very uncomplicated either.

'Thanks for doing this. You being here means a lot to my mum. She was so pleased to see you.'

'I think it was you she was happy to see—seriously, I'm just icing.' Kara started to unpack her bag, but kept her voice low. 'Declan, why haven't you done reconstruction on her scars?'

'Don't you think I've tried? Don't you think I've offered to bring her to London and get her the best treatment available? She doesn't want to. She says she's come to terms with it and I just have to accept that. I became a plastic surgeon just so I could help her, but she's not interested.'

And even though he tried to bite down his frustration Kara noticed. Taking his hand in hers, she pulled him to sit on the bed.

'I understand—I do. But I guess you have to let it go. If she's come to terms with it, then so should you. She's not an invalid—she's a grown woman who clearly must know what she's doing if she's brought all you kids up.'

Kara didn't know the half of it.

'It's other things she's struggled with.' And he couldn't bring himself to explain. He didn't want to even *think* about his father and the legacy he'd left.

Nothing about this place had any kind of reminder of his dad. Declan had made sure of that.

Kara's hand ran down his spine in soft strokes that almost undid him. 'I really hope your family like me. They seem lovely. All of them.'

'You haven't met all of them yet…that will be an experience. You did bring earplugs?'

'For sleeping?'

'No, for dinner. Don't say I didn't warn you.'

He grinned at her knotted brow and ached to smooth it over with his mouth. To wrap her in his arms and lie there surrounded by all the smells and sounds of home—the familiar, but with Kara, so exotic and different.

'It gets busy, but it's a family rule that we all eat together.'

'That's nice. I don't remember many meals like that growing up. It was usually just me and one of my parents, or a nanny, or a grandparent, and then as I got older, when I came home for the holidays, it was often just me and a TV dinner.'

At her words his stomach tightened—because although he'd made a space for himself far away he couldn't imagine growing up sitting at an empty dinner table in silence, or with only the TV for company. For him dinner had always meant chatter and good food and just the occasional argument. No wonder she'd grabbed the chance of marriage so young, to create a feeling of belonging.

She looked around the room, at the high ceiling and the intricate coving he'd designed. 'Did you really try to build this place?'

He laughed. 'Yes. I had a hand in all the buildings. This is a converted barn. It didn't get damaged much in the fire, so I just had it renovated to my specs. But I had more of a go at building the main house. Pretty naive, but when you're that young you think you can do everything.'

'And the great Declan Underwood *can't*? You do surprise me.'

It hadn't been for lack of trying. 'It soon became apparent that it was better for me to work as a doctor and pay someone else to do the physical work. As I earnt more we added more buildings—the barns, Niamh's house out back, the milking shed… But I did some labouring in my spare time.'

Dark memories slid through him. The smoke and the flames, the fear that had gripped his chest, the rough thick clutch at his throat as he'd tried to breathe in a furnace.

Then the days, months, years of dealing with scars, betrayal, grief. And finally restoration.

'Wow, that's some responsibility you carried here. Did you work with your dad?'

'No. He left.'

She frowned. 'So it really was just you? On your own?'

'Yep. Me and the builders, obviously…and the architects…' And the insurance. And the… Hell, there'd been a lot of professionals involved. Just not the one person he'd needed.

'But who did you ask for help? Who gave you advice?'

Would she not let it go? 'I didn't need any.'

'Everyone needs someone to talk things through with, Declan. Even you. Do you still have contact with your dad?'

'No.'

Once he'd been unable to leave his father's side, had looked to him for everything. To learn how to do the practical things for running a farm. How to be a decent farmer. A decent man. And then...

He swallowed back the bile rising in his throat. 'I wouldn't want anything from him now.'

'Why not?'

'Forget him, Kara. I have.'

He'd tried to erase the memories. The ones where his father had carried his boy high on his shoulders. The ones where they'd been fishing, hunting, laughing. Memories he didn't want because they weren't real. Oh, yes, he'd believed them then—but after his father had left he'd realised they were meaningless. Because love wasn't real—it was fleeting and flimsy and disposable. *That* was the one true thing he'd learnt from his father.

He looked at Kara, sitting there, not a memory. She was real, here, in front of him, and he grew hard just looking at that mouth, those eyes, that body. He wanted her, and that urgent feral response threatened to subsume him.

'So all that hard physical work explains these, then.'

Her hand slid to his biceps and a river of desire ran through him. When her hand slipped to his chest and her fingers brushed against his abs he was lost.

'And these too...'

That brief touch was like a spark to an ember. The next thing he knew he was leaning her back across the four-poster bed and planting kisses on her lips, on her cheeks and the sweet sun-blushed skin at her throat. And she was kissing him back—not hesitantly, not softly, but with all the intensity of a woman who needed kissing. Who wanted to be thoroughly kissed.

And that was what he told himself as he stroked his tongue in her mouth and felt her meld her body against his. *She wanted this.* As he peeled away the cardigan and dropped it to the floor, as he undid the tiny buttons on her blouse and unclipped the scrap of pure white lace that pretended to be a bra—because, by God, it was barely covering her straining breasts. *She wanted this.*

When he took her hardened nipple in his mouth and felt her moan into his hair. When she straddled him and rocked against his erection. When she kissed him hot and greedy and needy with her slick wet mouth.

Her hands were dragging his shirt away, her nails scraping along his back. Her mouth was kissing trails down his ribcage, her hair a mess of blonde against his chest. But it was her eyes that told him most, glittering dark like the most precious emeralds. *She wanted this.*

And, *God*, so did he. He wanted to be inside Kara right now—to ride her to the edge and back. To wipe away that half-smile and replace it with a sexy, satiated one. He wanted to watch her come, to taste her, to feel her clamp around him, to wake up with her in the morning. Because they had forty-eight hours to find each other before things were back on an even keel in a world where they didn't do complicated.

But in reality losing himself in Kara wasn't complicated at all. It was the simplest thing he'd ever done.

CHAPTER TEN

KISS ME. SHE was so on the edge of giving herself up to him.

And she didn't want it just to stop there.

But Kara heard the sound of footsteps and
giggles outside the door and pulled away from
Declan, naked from the waist up. Suddenly she
felt cold—and not just physically naked but psychologically laid bare too. Because making love
with him would confuse everything. Kissing him
like this had already stirred enough chaos in her
brain.

She rested her forehead against his and laughed.
'This sneaking around behind closed doors makes
me feel like a teenager again.'

'Unfortunately that's the way it is here—no
damned privacy. Even this far away from the
house.'

He was still hard, she could feel him underneath her, but he didn't appear to mind. He just

seemed content to stroke his fingers down the curve of her body.

'But I think it's dinnertime. We'd best get dressed and get down there. Hungry?'

Yes, but not for food. 'You bet.'

Fastening her bra and grabbing another top from her weekend bag, Kara made herself presentable. It was weird having him watch her do such an intimate thing that no one had seen her do since her marriage. Even weirder as he brushed by and kissed the top of her head, sheathing that gorgeous body back into his shirt. It all seemed so natural for him, this playing at being a couple. And for her it felt…strange. Connected and yet disconnected.

One thing was for sure: having seen him seminaked, she was definitely going to miss that body when she went back to London and back to her old team.

'So, does your mum do the cooking for you all? That must be a mission.'

'Mostly. There was a time when she couldn't manage, so Niamh helped, but she's better now. Well…'

Once again something flickered behind his

eyes and she wanted to ask Declan his story. Because while his mother might well be healed he still carried scars in his need to protect her.

'She seems just a little shy, Declan, that's all. But, hey, I don't know her, so I don't want to be talking out of turn.' She changed the subject, not wanting to start the visit off on the wrong footing. 'So, dinner…?'

'Can wait just a few more seconds. I have something much more interesting in mind…'

He pushed her against the door and kissed her again, this time gently, like a summer breeze against her lips, his hands cradling her face. And she kissed him back, determining to enjoy the next couple of days instead of analysing them. They both knew this couldn't go any further than a little flirtation, and she was big enough to deal with that.

The dining room was dominated by a large mahogany table and a selection of matching chairs, bright plastic highchairs and a long wooden bench. A glass chandelier gave off a subdued pearly glow. At one end of the room a large stone fireplace promised cosy winter nights, and all round the room on various dressers and book-cases were photos: a teenage Declan and his sisters, the babies, a selection of gruff-looking mongrel dogs, the farm, visitors.

As none of the pictures was of the siblings when very young, Kara suspected these had all been taken post-fire. 'Did you lose a lot of stuff in the fire?'

'Most everything. The house was pretty de-stroyed, but there were a few things we managed to save. No photos, though.'

'None of your mum? *Mam?*' Kara wanted to fit in, but the word didn't roll off her tongue just yet. She picked up a photo of Declan aged about sixteen, grinning wildly with a stack of bricks on a hod, then glanced at another of him in gradua-tion gown and cap. 'My, my, how you've grown.'

'I damn well hope so. I was a wiry little whip-per back then. And, no, she won't have any taken. She says she doesn't want to ruin the pictures.'

'But that's such a shame.' She bit back a ques-tion about Declan's father. No photos of him ei-ther.

'Dinner's ready,' Niamh announced, bounding

in with a large casserole dish in her hands and a bottle of wine tucked under one arm.

Declan strode forward and took it from his sister. 'Careful.'

'Don't you love the macho? And the manners? Where did they come from? I think you've knocked some sense into my brother, Kara. It's about time someone did.' Niamh leaned towards her. 'So, the others are here. Take a deep breath and then let it out very slowly…oh, and take a big slug of wine to help calm your nerves. Let the chaos begin!'

And within a second Kara was enveloped in hugs and hands and smiling faces, her ears filled with musical names and lyrical-sounding words. She was found a seat next to Declan, given a plate filled with steaming chunks of meat covered in a dark rich gravy, large mounds of creamy mashed potatoes and a glass of red. And she was smiling with Aoife, laughing at Roisin's tales of medical school, feeding one of the little ones in a highchair, and everything under the protective gaze of Declan. It was exhausting, but lovely.

'So, Declan's never brought a girl home before. Spill the beans…how did you two meet?'

It was Briana, the romantic of the family. She'd already told Kara about her dream wedding dress, the honeymoon, the number of babies she'd have. All she needed to do was find the right man. Kara didn't say anything about her own past, wanting Briana to hold on tight to her dreams, because every girl deserved them.

'At work—well, kind of…'

Declan grinned as his foot connected with Kara's under the table. His toes slid up her leg until she realised she must have been grinning like an…how did he say it? An *eejit*. An intense sexual need ran through her veins.

Then his hand shifted over to her lap and his fingers tiptoed towards her thigh. She squirmed in her seat.

'At a ball, no less. Kara wore a long gold gown and taught me a few Aussie swear words and a drinking game…a lot of tequila was involved. I knew immediately that she was the girl for me.'

And he grinned his goofy grin and made it sound, truly, as if they were made for each other. He never mentioned how she'd left him standing on the dance floor after a searing kiss that had turned her legs to jelly and her brain to mush.

And heaven knew what they were doing here—doing this. Because she didn't have a clue. Except that she wished his hands were running over every part of her.

'Ah, a ball…every girl's dream. So romantic.' Briana clapped her hands together. 'And the wedding?'

Whoa. Kara spluttered into her wine as she felt Declan's grip on her thigh tighten.

'Has not been discussed.'

'Leave it alone, Bri. They don't need you meddling in their business. Remember, Kara's our guest. Be polite.'

Declan's mother's voice soothed the conversation. Kara realised the older woman had been observing, but hadn't actually spoken until now. Everyone stilled and looked at her with surprise. Was it so unusual for her to contribute to a conversation?

'Kara, tell us, have you visited Ireland before?'

'No. Not at all, apparently I have ancestors here somewhere—County Wicklow, I think. I can't wait to have a sticky bea…a good look round tomorrow. Declan said he'd take me for a drive.'

'A drive?' Briana looked horrified. 'I thought

he'd be teaching you how to milk cows. You know, in the cowshed…' Now she winked. 'Down and dirty…'

'Briana! You have a dirty mind,' Niamh interjected. 'Er…how about a spot of shopping? I could come with you.'

'We thought we'd take a look at the city on the way back to the airport on Sunday,' Kara answered, turning her head this way and that to speak to them all. 'He knows a good pub that sells great food.'

'Sure, Dec knows all the pubs with the best *craic*,' added Roisin with a wink. As the baby of the family, she clearly adored her big brother.

Uh-oh. Dictionary required. 'What's crack?'

'Craic.' Roisin laughed. 'It means fun. A laugh. There's plenty of it in Dublin. And while you're there you could come have a look round the Trinity College campus. It's beautiful. Actually, you could give me a ride back there on Sunday.'

'What about a horse-ride? There's a trail over the hills that takes you down to the river—it's pretty special.' Aoife joined in, her hand never leaving that of her quiet fiancé, Ronan, and soon everyone had voiced their ideas of how to entertain an out-of-town guest.

Kara looked to Declan for an opinion, taking comfort in the fact that his hand was still on her lap and that the spotlight had moved on from their nuptials. His smile was slow and made her stomach flutter. She got the impression, with the smouldering heat in his eyes, that Declan's idea of entertaining his out-of-town guest was nothing at all to do with going out and everything to do with staying in.

'Whatever you want, Kara.'

I want you. She swallowed deeply, wondering just how much deeper she had to fall before she could harden herself to him completely. 'Wow, there are so many fabulous things to do here. I'll let you decide.'

When Declan squeezed her thigh...this time higher...much higher...Kara almost choked on her white chocolate and raspberry cheesecake.

Afterwards, when everyone was helping to clear up in the kitchen, Kara offered to help but was flatly refused. Irish hospitality, she supposed.

'Okay, but it's the party tomorrow, is that right?

What do we do? What do I need to bring? Do you need help with anything?'

Niamh gently held her by the shoulders. 'No. Absolutely not. Now, we've a few things to do in here, but you go and sit down. Tomorrow you can do some sightseeing, and in the evening we'll have a cake.'

'Here, have another drink. It helps. Trust me, I know.'

Declan topped up Kara's glass while jiggling the small child sitting on his shoulders up and down. For all his self-imposed exile he'd managed to slip right back in and seemed, despite himself, to be enjoying his time here.

Because, whatever Declan said to the contrary, he was a family man through and through. She could see that from the pure joy in his eyes as he piggybacked each child in turn, as he lost himself deep in conversation with Roisin about her grades, as he watched his mother with a look in his eyes that spoke of his regret and a fierce love.

'Wait! Just wait a minute—let me get my camera. I so need to remember all of this.'

Kara dashed out to the barn and back and took a series of snaps of Declan with a variety of relatives and ankle-biters playing the fool, flicking each other with washing up foam. And then one with all the siblings looking reasonably decent and the children smiling. Mostly.

'Now, *that's* one for the album.'

Out of the corner of her eye she caught Mary watching, her eyes guarded, her shyness now morphing into embarrassment about being caught on camera. Kara raised her eyebrows in question...*do you want to join in*? But Mary turned away and shoved her hands in the soapy water.

So Kara got snap-happy with the rest of the family, clicking and laughing and showing the children all the photos she was taking—making them stick out their tongues, pull their best crazy faces, joining in with them to cries of, *'Again! Again!'* It seemed that she'd get tired of it long before they would.

A little later, when Declan approached his mum and she lifted her head to him and smiled, Kara clicked and caught a picture of them that, when she looked in the viewer, made her heart ache. From this angle, even though her face was in full view, the only thing that shone out was the deep love between the two of them. If only Mary could understand that everyone saw past her scars, and that the only person she was hiding from, really, was herself.

Suddenly Niamh grabbed the camera and Kara realised she was in the spotlight once again. 'Wait. Let's get one of the happy couple. Quick, Dec, get your arm around that lovely girl's shoulder. That's right. Great. Now smile.'

Happy couple. The idea thrilled inside Kara... and frightened her to death. Every instinct in her fought against being another half of something— something that might subsume her, something that would spiral out of control. And yet...

'Come here, then.'

Declan wrapped his arm round her and looked down into her eyes. And she could feel herself falling and falling into his gaze and his smile and his heat. She tried to smile too, but the whirl of emotions running through her stretched her too far. She wanted him. Wanted this. Wanted to have the dream, have everything.

But the harsh reality of it was that she'd fallen so hard for someone before...the wrong someone. And her dream had shattered into a million pieces along with her life. She couldn't do that again. Didn't know if she had the strength to pick herself up at the end.

Because how the hell did you ever know who the right someone was?

The walk back to the cottage was filled with things unsaid. The memory of his hand on her thigh lingered, turning from an ache to a need. He was close now—so close she could smell him again, that rich, earthy scent that was just him, mixed with a decent slug of red wine and white chocolate. Irresistible.

And maybe it was the wine, maybe it was the fresh Irish air, but her guard and her sense seemed to leech from her with every step closer to the cottage.

As they reached her bedroom door he looked down at her with eyes that held a zillion promises. 'You have everything you need?'

'Yes. Thanks.' *Except you.*

It was a pure physical ache. She wanted to pull him inside and drag him onto the bed again. But instead she demurely waited for him to invite himself in—it was his house after all. And she didn't know the rules. What would it cost her to be able to give a little of herself for two nights with him? She didn't want to think.

'Thanks for a lovely evening.'

His head was close to hers now, his hand against the door. But he didn't come in and close it as he had before. 'You certainly bowled them over.'

'Oh, you know…I have a gift.'

'So do I.'

He ran a finger down her cheek, making her insides melt. Hot and needy. How could one touch make her ache with so much want?

'Oh…' She spoke through a dry throat, her hand on his chest feeling the sharp erratic rise and fall of his breath. 'And what would that be?'

'You'll have to wait and see.'

'Spoilsport.'

He came into the room and closed the door. She inhaled sharply. Declan. The bed. Night. Reality hit her like a tornado. 'Are you…staying in here tonight?'

'You know, you ask way too many questions.'

His mouth was on her neck, sending ripples of need through her.

'Do you want me to?'

Yes. No. She didn't know. She was scared.

Scared about what would happen if she gave herself to him. Scared about what would happen if she didn't.

'Oh, God, that feels so good.'

'You're very tense. Here, relax.' He sat her on the bed, knelt behind her and massaged her shoulders. Smoothly, slowly, rhythmically. Until she rocked under his hands, drifting from pleasure to some kind of daydream until she didn't know which was which.

His breath was on her neck. Heating her. 'I'm sorry, I know we can be a bit overwhelming. But the hard bit's over now—they've met you and you've survived.'

'It's not them. It's…this. I don't know what we're doing.' She went for her trademark forthright and hoped she didn't sound needy. She'd spent way too much time in her marriage trying to fathom out what was going on and never quite being able to work it out. From then on she'd determined never to be left in some kind of relationship darkness. 'Declan, why am I here?'

'Because you are very…very…lovely.' His mouth was on that soft spot of her shoulder that made her curl into him, and it would have been so easy to let him carry on. So, so easy.

She pulled away. 'No, really. That wasn't what I was asking. I don't want you to give me compliments. I want some truths. Really, why am I here?'

Declan's hands dropped to his sides. His eyes closed for a beat. Two. Good question. God knew why she was here, save for the fact he'd wanted something else to think about during the birthday weekend.

He could hear the *thud-thud* of his heart echoing in his ears. He searched for words. Found himself wanting.

But she deserved some kind of explanation. 'All my life I've worked to give them the things they want, that they deserve. The things my father didn't. Everything I did was to provide security and a future. And I'd do it all again in a heartbeat. But being back here always feels so… tying. So claustrophobic. I can't breathe.'

It wasn't just the people, but the memories. Dark emotions filled his chest.

'Sometimes London isn't far away enough…

but I thought if I brought you along we could have some fun. Lighten things up a bit. I really do want to show you the place.'

And put some sort of distance between himself and his family.

Her eyes widened and he wanted to jump deep into them and never resurface.

'They're a handful, all right. But isn't that what families are like? Especially big ones like yours. Your mum deserves a medal to have had you all.'

'She deserves more than that. The things she went through...' It made his heart hurt and re-inforced his determination never to get close to anyone.

So why he was sitting here, sharing this with Kara, he couldn't fathom. Part of him wanted to tell her everything. The other half wanted to run a mile—away from this proximity, from this feeling that somehow she might fit. Seeing his mother so betrayed by love had made him try to harden his heart. Hell, he hadn't had to try too hard. Watching his father walk away, refusing to turn to his wife's pleas and his son's desperate words, had cemented a block of ice in his chest.

He couldn't let it melt now. Talking to her, sharing things like this with her, would open him up to the risk of being hurt again.

'So tell me, Declan. What happened?'

Nonsensically, and the opposite of what he should have done, he silenced her with a kiss. The feel of her mouth underneath his sent spasms of need zipping through him. He wanted to erase the past, to create a new present that was just Kara and him. Wanted to fill his senses with her. She tasted sweet, like the cheesecake, hot as fire and soft. So soft beneath him. She smelt of freedom and heat and home and a foreign land he wanted to explore.

He pulled her close. When she opened her mouth he thought she was going to ask more questions. Whatever else happened, he was all out of talking. 'No. Not now, Kara.'

'Yes. Now.' Her hands were on his chest, fingers fisting the fabric of his shirt. And he realised, with a surge of heat in his gut, that she was not talking about the same thing he was.

CHAPTER ELEVEN

ALMOST REVERENTLY HE peeled Kara's clothes off. When she tried to unzip his jeans he stopped her hand. 'No. You first.'

And this time there was no embarrassment, no chill, as his hands stroked her from shoulder to waist or when he stood apart from her and looked. Just looked, with such pure intensity that she believed his words. The lump returned to her throat.

'My God, Kara, you are so beautiful. So, so beautiful.'

Then he was holding her close again, lips clamped to hers, and she feverishly tasted him, savoured him. She moaned when he dragged his mouth away. Moaned more when he pressed it against her neck. Her chest. Her nipple.

Silently he scooped her up into his arms and carried her to the bed. Whatever doubts she'd had until this moment were forgotten. She would have him. Because she couldn't not. This moment was meant to happen and she had no strength or desire to fight it. Her thoughts were muddled, but so clear. Bad idea. Good idea. All she knew was that she had to have him.

Her hands moved to his chest, ripping each button apart until she was feeling skin. Hot muscle under her fingers. She leant him back on the duvet and straddled him, relishing the hardness beneath her. Knowing that every single ache in her body was mirrored in his. Mirrored too in eyes that had lost their soulfulness, that were not teasing or playful but intense and dark and urgent.

'Kara, we don't have to—'

'Yes, we do.' She leant forward and kissed him again, arching against the hands now circling her bottom. Slowly, slowly his fingers trailed up and across her abdomen, making her catch her breath in short staggered gasps. Then his thumbs brushed her nipples, followed by his mouth. Hot and greedy, he licked as each bud hardened under his touch.

His jaw was stubbled and it burnt across her chest, and she enjoyed the raw feel of him, stoking a fierce need. Not listening any more to his resistance, she unzipped his jeans, shucked them to the floor and took him in her hand.

'Wait. Kara, wait.'

'I need you.'

She heard the words, heeded the emotion. Didn't care. Didn't care that she had opened herself to him in every way—to hurt, to pain. Because that would be some time in the future and this was now. *He* was now. And she didn't want to think about the past or some time not yet happened. She wanted to live this moment.

'God, Declan. I need you so much.'

Furious and fast, he sheathed, and then she was lowering herself onto him. His body was slick and hard. And she was ready for him. Had been ready for so long. As he entered her she gasped. Heat engulfed her, filled her.

Turning her onto her back, he murmured her name, thrusting deep and slow. Too slow. Too fast. Her mind was a chaotic whirl. Her body was responding to his scent, his touch. This was perfect. He was perfect.

And then he was harder, faster, and more perfect than she could even imagine, and she felt herself falling again. Falling deeper and deeper, and flying higher. Soaring. Until she was…he was…they were lost. Lost somewhere on the edge of forever. Somewhere deep in the core of her heart.

'Now, here's the gift I was telling you about last night.' Declan brought out the large parcel he'd hidden in the bottom of his luggage and handed it to Kara in the farmyard.

The breeze had dropped and the early morning sun glinted off her hair, highlighting the gold. As she pulled her silver-grey cardigan around her and stamped her skinny-jean-wrapped legs he didn't think he'd seen anything so breathtaking.

And yet…

Her eyebrows rose. And was that a flicker of uncertainty behind those eyes?

Definitely. The smile she gave him was hesitant. She fiddled again with the hem of her cardigan, as she'd done the evening they'd arrived. Forthright Kara seemed to have developed a little more vulnerability, and she wore it in the dusky smudges beneath her eyes.

This was new ground. Complicated and unsteady. And if she felt anything like he did, then, man, they were in trouble. Because he didn't know the next step.

Friends? Lovers now? What? He'd never wanted any woman so deeply, or taken anyone with such need and intensity. Or wanted to stay and leave at the same time. No, he'd never wanted to stay before, and that was what spooked him the most. But he'd brought her here and he had to give her a good time for what was left of the weekend.

'Well, thank you, Declan. You mean you really do have a gift? I thought you were referring to… those other things.'

'Well, I know you have a passion for *these* kind of things, and I imagine you haven't got anything quite like them. But, believe me, you're going to need them.'

Confusion ran behind those green eyes as she ripped open the box and then tipped back her head and laughed. 'Gumboots? *Leprechaun* gumboots?' She held them up and turned them around and around as she took in the little grinning green men on the boots. 'Will I go all diddly -diddly now?'

'God forbid. The world is not ready for that.

Please, stay a diddly-free zone.' He helped her take off her very unsuitable black patent pumps and steadied her as she slid her legs into her new rubber boots. 'Wellies. Topboots. Waterboots. Not a gum in sight.'

'I love them. But for…?'

She gave him a twirl, kicked up one foot then the other. Pretty damned hot. And since when had he ever thought a woman in wellies could be hot?

'Milking. You don't get to come on a farm weekend for free, you know. There's something needed in return.'

Dark eyes blinked. 'You mean last night wasn't enough?'

'Last night was…more than enough.'

It had left something indelibly etched on his heart. Something he couldn't shake. Something he wanted to shake—because if he didn't he wasn't sure how he'd get out whole.

Without encouraging any more conversation along that line, he led her into a shed and climbed onto a dirt-splattered motorbike. The only way he knew how to clear his head. Then he pointed to the back, small as it was. 'Your chariot, my lady. I'll give you a backie down the field. We herd them up, bring them to the milking shed, then take them down again. Then we come back and hose the shed out.'

She looked at the bike, a little disappointed. 'This is nothing like the one in London. That is big and black and shiny and there's room for two. This is…shabby.'

'It is a bit grubby, I guess. But it's a nippy little fella. Come on—hold on tight.'

'There's no space.'

'Squeeze on. You'll be fine.' He pushed himself as far forward as he dared, and she slid right where he liked her best: hugging tight against his body, her legs wrapped round him, this time with no helmets, her hair flowing free in the wind.

With a roar he took her over the rough terrain, through divets and dips to the highest point of the hill and the deepest part of the valley. Fast. And he heard her squeal and screech, and he felt her arms tighten around his waist as the early morning chill bit into his cheeks.

When they reached the bottom of the hill she climbed off and dragged in a breath, pushing that silky blonde hair behind her ears. 'My God, that was wild.'

'You can drive on the way back if you like.'

'Oh, I don't know. I don't think so.'

'It's okay. I'll show you. It's not difficult.' Focus on something else. Anything to exorcise the confusion swirling in his gut right now. He took hold of the handlebar. 'Hop back on.'

Her eyes were sharp as she watched him. 'Maybe. I don't know. I think I might be better as a passenger.'

'I taught the girls before—you'll be fine. Give it a go.' He twisted the key and started the bike up. 'This side is the clutch and gears. The right side is brake and accelerator.'

He showed her a couple of times, until she got the hang of moving forward in first gear and quickly changing up to second.

'Go.'

Off she flew with a scream, stuttering and bunny-hopping, legs flapping out at the sides, then came to a juddering halt. 'Help!'

'Squeeze gently and slowly—there. See? You're getting the hang of it.'

He watched the flurry of hair, the cosmopolitan dressed form buzzing round the field—his life in London and his life in Ireland suddenly melding into one.

His heart jerked.

She had derailed him. Totally. His body knew how to react, but his brain was definitely, seriously spooked.

When she came back over the hill and drew to a halt her back wheel skidded in an arc. Mud churned like his thoughts, spraying him in dirt. 'Hey! Watch it.'

'Oops. Sorry!'

Not sorry at all, she clambered off, her hand over her laughing mouth, head tipped back. He watched the gentle curve of her neck, the movement of her delicate throat as she spoke.

'Told you I'd be rubbish.'

'No, you didn't. And you're not. You're a natural… Well, with a little practice.'

For a second their eyes caught, lost in the fun, lost in the moment. The urge to kiss her again was almost unbearable. He wanted to taste her, touch her. To put his mouth on those places he'd explored last night. To wake up with her again.

But this time he wanted that waking to be joy-filled, not loaded with confusion.

As her laughter died on her lips questions formed in her eyes. Questions he couldn't answer. Questions he didn't want to be asked. And he knew that when they got back to real life nothing would be the same again.

'Okay.' He found his voice. 'So, let's get on with the milking. Everyone'll be waiting for us back at the house.'

Pushing all other thoughts aside, he instructed her in the best way to deal with the cows up close, but he was trying to keep a distance. Trying to keep a goddamned distance between friendship and something beyond intense.

'So this is the place where I grew up. Not much more than a village, really.'

Declan walked Kara along the cobbled main street of one of the prettiest places she'd ever visited.

The road was flanked with quaint shopfronts painted in pastels: pink, blue and white. Tiny flags wove across the road and back again; flowers adorned each windowsill. It was like something from a film, from the last century, from centuries ago.

'Gosh, it's so beautiful. How could you ever leave?'

'Because it's tiny and there's nothing here for me. At least not job-wise.'

'Well, maybe you should have built a hospital as well as your houses and barns.'

He laughed, a little more relaxed now, she noticed, as they'd put distance between themselves and the farm. But there was still an edge there, and she couldn't help thinking it had a lot to do with last night.

'Steady now, girl. I'm not Superman.'

'Well, really? That's a shame. There was me thinking...'

He looked at her quizzically and there was a warning in his voice not to mention last night. 'Thinking what?'

Actually, once again she hadn't been thinking at all. Not thinking when she'd lain in his arms, when she'd taken him inside her and almost wept at the pleasure. Not thinking about tomorrow, or being back at work, or how she would extricate her heart from all of this when the time came.

Her heart. *Huh.* She tried to put everything into perspective. It was only sex. That was all. Natural and normal. The logical conclusion of attraction.

It wasn't…couldn't…be more than that.

'Ah, nothing.'

Heat flared in her chest at the realisation that it could be, might be, more than that, and she fished around for something to distract her—something that wasn't him and the thought of last night. Of how amazing he'd made her feel.

Glancing across the road, she saw a pharmacy. 'Hey, I've had a thought. Why don't we print off some of those photos I took last night and put them in a frame for your mum? I got some good pictures. I'm sure she'll like them.'

He looked bemused, but shrugged. 'You don't think the scarf you bought her is enough for a birthday present?'

'Well, it can be a thank-you-for-having-me gift instead, then. Or an extra present from you, if you like?' She hesitated to say *from us*. 'I don't want those lovely pictures to go to waste when all they'll do is stay on my laptop.'

She dragged him into the pharmacy and handed over the camera's memory card. Then they meandered through the shops along the main street while they waited for the photos to print.

Presently they came across an antiques shop. Inside was a cornucopia of old-style Ireland. Wicker baskets and old rusted irons, heavy wooden furniture and cloth embroidered in Celtic symbols. Nothing like Declan's place, but everything like his mum's.

Kara pointed to a silver picture frame with spaces for three photographs. 'Look, that's beautiful. Let's buy that.'

'Why?' he asked later as they sat in a café flicking through the prints. 'Why are you doing this?'

'Why not? Declan, you've got a lovely family here. I just want to celebrate it.' She showed him a picture of the little ones sticking out their tongues and laughed. 'How about this? Or this…?'

It was the photo of him and his mum in the kitchen.

'This. This one definitely.'

He shook his head, his mouth a grim line. 'I told you, she doesn't do photos.'

'Why? She looks beautiful in this. Look at it. You can't see her scars—all you can see is a very proud woman who has survived.' Kara's heart squeezed. 'Give it to her, Declan. I'm sure she'll love it. Would you give a decent photo to Niamh or Briana?'

'I guess.' Shaking his head, he hauled in oxygen. 'I just never really...'

'Really what?'

He didn't look at her. 'Could see past those damned scars.'

And if he felt almost responsible for them being there Kara could understand that. But if he was looking for absolution then she wasn't the one to give it. It had to come from within him.

She was beginning to understand just what made it difficult for Declan to get close to anyone. Responsibility wasn't just about giving things to people, it was about risking your heart with them...and he couldn't do that. He'd been hurt badly, she thought, and he was all about protecting his family. But most of all himself.

'But if you can't see past them then how the hell will she?'

For a few moments he stared into his coffee cup. Kara couldn't read him. The day had been dotted with moments of reflection—him, her.

She could see him building the barriers between them again.

'Okay, you're right. I'll give it to her. Thanks.'

She wanted to reach over and kiss a smile back on to his face. She'd lost count now of the kisses. 'So, what's on the agenda now?'

'Ah...' His eyes glittered and he shook off his mood. 'I'm torn between washing down the slurry pit or—'

'No way. You brought me here to do some sightseeing, not deal with cow poo.'

'You didn't let me finish...' Now his eyes positively sizzled with promise. '*Or* we could just go back to the cottage?'

He didn't need to explain any further. An afternoon in bed with Declan certainly appealed. Hell, she couldn't think of anything she'd rather do. There was only one night left, after all, before they went back to being colleagues.

Picking up the pictures, he secured three into the frame and went to put the rest back in the envelope. One dropped out onto the table between them.

The one Niamh had taken. *The happy couple.* Kara gasped. The way she looked up at Declan, her body turned into his, her arm secured around his waist, head tilted...the smile that laid open her heart. And the way his hand lay across her shoulder, possessive—but adoring.

God. Her heart felt as if it was rubbed raw. Was that how they looked to everyone else? Truly, heart-stoppingly, gut-wrenchingly connected?

Panic rose from her stomach and tightened like a vice. This couldn't happen.

She couldn't feel like that—as if he was meant for her. As if this time—*this time*—things might work.

She couldn't allow her heart to be blown wide-open again.

She cleared her throat. 'I'm thinking horse-riding might be nice. Or we could babysit the kids while Niamh goes shopping.'

Anything. Anything that would stop her getting closer, falling deeper, losing herself further in Declan Underwood.

CHAPTER TWELVE

'MAM LOVES THE pictures. Thank you.' Declan found Kara sitting on a wooden bench in the garden, illuminated only by thick yellow moonlight.

He'd done his duty and given his mum more attention than she'd ever wanted, had helped around the farm and managed a horse-ride with Kara. Now the birthday cake had been cut and eaten and his family had settled down to watch a movie.

And he just needed a little distance from everyone. Except Kara. Seemed he couldn't keep distance from her no matter how much he tried.

Curling her wellie-clad feet underneath her bottom, she smiled. 'See. I told you she'd like them.'

'You know, I never realised just how much stronger she'd become over the years.'

'Well, Niamh would say it's because you don't get over to see her enough. But I'd say it's because you treat her the same way you always have. With respect, but pity too.' Kara shifted as he sat next to her. 'She doesn't need that now.'

'And you're always right?'

She nodded and her hair bobbed around her face. 'Obviously.'

'And smug too.'

'Takes one to know one.' She turned to look at him and wrinkled her nose as she smiled. 'I was meaning to ask you—why didn't you take over the family business, become a farmer like your dad?'

He cleared his throat as he tried to counteract the instinctive stiffening of his muscles at the mention of his father. 'No money in it. Not really. I needed something else, something more. Something…a long way from here.'

'You know, every time I mention your dad you close up just a little bit more.'

Busted. 'Bluntness just rolls off you, eh? You're not exactly one of those meek conformist women, are you?'

She shrugged. 'Believe me, I've tried and tried to fit my big cuboid persona into a round hole. And failed. Too many times to count.'

'Oh?'

She nibbled at her bottom lip and he could see her weighing up what to say. Silence stretched. He understood why she'd prefer to keep her secrets, but that didn't mean he didn't want to hear them.

'Too many times...?'

She sighed and peered straight ahead, her fingers gripped tightly together. 'Rob thought I should have been different... Well, let's just say I was a huge disappointment to him.'

'How could you ever be a disappointment?'

She shrugged. 'We started out wanting the same things, or at least I thought we did. But after he joined up he changed. He became more demanding, more possessive and authoritarian. It was his way or no way. He'd always said he was going to stay in the army for a few years, then get out...but that changed and he wanted to stay on for longer and longer. It was all about him and nothing about what I wanted or the dreams we'd made together. And I wasn't allowed to complain. Just comply.'

'So what? He wanted a divorce? Or...? Don't tell me he hurt you?' Acid rose in his stomach as he fought an intense primal anger at the thought of anyone laying a finger on Kara's perfect body.

She shook her head, her voice unsteady. 'Not physically. But the pressure was there always…to be the perfect wife, to do what was expected, not to ask for anything that I wanted, not to expect better…or more. God, I tried so hard to make it work. I wanted it all so badly. I wanted the dream. It was there, all I had to do was step into it, and yet…it wasn't a dream at all. I thought if I tried to love him more it would be enough love for both of us.'

Declan's gut contracted. The man had clearly been an idiot. 'You were so young, though. How did you even know what you were doing?'

'Yeah. Pretty tragic to realise at twenty-two years old that you've made the biggest mistake of your life and you're stuck. That you are way better at working than you are at loving.' She squeezed her hands together in her lap. 'I believed those vows, Declan. I loved him. I committed myself to him for life.' Her eyes glistened. 'Hard to admit it, but I was—plain and simple— married to the wrong man. It took me a long time to figure it out.'

Hell, he'd seen that before—right here in these damned fields, in what became a pile of smouldering ash. 'You didn't leave?'

Her brows came together. 'I didn't want to face the truth. I had enough trouble reconciling that sometimes love just isn't enough to keep two people together. I couldn't actually put voice to that fact.' She sighed. 'And when he died it all seemed such a waste—he could have been happier without me, with someone else.'

His stomach hit his boots. He imagined her as a teenager in a wedding dress, living a dream. The harsh reality she'd faced when it had crumbled around her despite how hard she'd worked to save it. So young. Too young.

Declan's heart jittered. He tipped up her chin and looked into her eyes. 'God, Kara, there are good men out there—men who will cherish and love you and who will willingly nurture you. But I do understand. I know enough about selfish men to write the goddamned book.'

'Your dad?' Her hand was at his cheek now.

Breathe. He nodded and stared out into the darkness. 'Yes, but let's just forget him too.'

She gave him a wobbly smile as she slid into

his open arms and leaned her head against his chest. This was supposed to be about her...just about her. She looked to him for some kind of understanding or absolution.

'Good to know I'm not the only messed-up one.'

'We're all messed up somehow, Kara. You'll be fine. You are more than fine. You're marvellous.' He squeezed her against him, then stood up, pulling her with him. 'Come on, let's walk and clear our heads. Think about what we could do tomorrow.'

He needed to get away from the house he'd tried to build with his bare hands because of a dumb-ass man who'd pleased no one but himself. So he grasped her fist and wandered through the fading light towards the open fields. He'd moved to London to get away from all this... He never shared this stuff—not with Leo or any of the Hunter Clinic guys, not with his friends. Memories were best left alone as far as he was concerned. Until they threatened to overwhelm you.

'Talk to me, Declan. Tell me about your dad.'

'No. It won't make you feel any better.'

She squeezed his hand, her voice less shaky now. 'It can't make me feel much worse. Can it?'

How blissfully ignorant she was. And she should stay that way. 'Look at the stars, Kara. A bit different to the sky in Australia?'

She tipped her head back and stared upwards. 'A little. It's bigger and brighter in Australia, is all. And the constellations are in a different place. Now, stop avoiding it.'

And, yes, that was what he'd done for years. Buried everything deep and got on with making a better life. A life that was so damned full he didn't have time for this…sharing and sentiment and drama. Yes, she had some—as he'd suspected. But instead of being irritating it had cut him deep.

She stopped dead and hugged her arms around him until most of her pressed against a lot of him. 'It's only fair. I've told you my guilty secrets—now it's your turn. And I'm not moving until you do.'

'That's not much of a threat. I like it like this. Very much.'

He took the opportunity to smooth his hands down her back and press her against a lot more of him. And wondered whether getting hard in the middle of an intense personal conversation was against someone's rules. Clearly not against his. But then, he never had personal conversations like this, so he could put it down to rookie error.

She dropped her hold and took two steps back. 'Okay…so no hugs until you talk.'

'Would you ever grow up?'

'No. I don't want to. Growing up sucks. As I found out to my cost.' The smile slipped. 'But I guess I'm the only one big enough to open my heart.'

And even though he knew about this kind of game, because his sisters had played it too many times, and even though he knew not to rise to her challenge, that once he'd started he'd find it hard to lock his anger away again, he felt the words rising within him. Because Kara had that way about her that made you want to tell her the truth.

He looked back up the hill towards the house, saw the light in the kitchen. Remembered how the light had filled him with terror that night. The light and the thick smoke, the crackle, the orange sparks rising into the black sky. An acrid smell that had filled his lungs.

'Dad had gone out for a drink that night—nothing unusual. *"You're in charge, boy,"* he'd said as he'd left. He always did that. It was our...' his voice cracked at the irony '...in joke. I was in my room and heard screaming from the lounge. My mum was yelling at me there was a fire and to get the girls out. Thick black smoke was everywhere. Heat. The smell. But I managed to get to them in the back bedroom and fought my way down with them. One by one.'

Kara's hand cupped her mouth. 'I can't imagine the terror.'

'I thought Mum was outside. But I couldn't find her. I called and tried to go back in but I couldn't breathe. I couldn't get to her. I tried. *Tried.* But the more I tried the hotter the flames and the thicker the smoke became. I couldn't breathe. I thought she'd be dead. I thought...I'd let her die. Then suddenly Dad was there, taking control, running in to what looked like a furnace. And then I thought I'd lose them both.'

And, to his eternal shame, he'd hoped and prayed that if the worst thing happened and only one person got out alive it would be his father.

'Then he strode out with her in his arms.'

Kara stroked his back as they walked down towards the stream at the bottom of the hill. 'You must have been so scared.'

Desperate. But his hero father had saved the day. At that moment the thirteen-year-old Declan had thought he couldn't love his father more.

'Mum was in and out of hospital. She was in pain, grew depressed and withdrawn with her injuries. And Dad didn't help. He couldn't look at her. Wouldn't tolerate her black moods. He began staying out more and more. Left me to do more of the work around the place—stayed out overnight. I wanted to ask him what we'd done wrong, why he didn't want to be around us. But the look in his eyes was so cold. And then one day he took me to one side and told me he'd met someone else so he was leaving. That was the last time I saw him.'

Kara shook her head against his heart. 'After everything you'd already been through…'

'In sickness and in health. That's what he promised. To love her. To love us all. Mum took it badly. She believed he left her because of her scars and it sent her spiralling into a black depression. I thought…I thought at one point she'd never get better. She was damaged. Devastated. And she thought it was all because of how she looked.'

He managed to bite back the bitterness he'd felt for so long.

'You don't walk away from the people you love, no matter what happens. Not if love means anything.'

Declan had grown up loving that man with every cell in his body. There'd been a bond, he'd thought, sacred between father and son.

Something inside him had broken the day his dad had left. And he'd had no idea how to fix it.

So he had buried his anger and disappointment and tried to turn it into something positive. Determined never to give anyone the chance to hurt him like that.

'But you know what? My mum didn't deserve that, and neither did the girls. If he wasn't prepared to provide for his family then I knew I had to man up and do it instead.'

And had done so every single day since.

The water babbled and gurgled, cutting through the thick silence of the night. His chest heaved as he fought back the memories, the fear and the anger.

Kara ran her fingers over his ribcage. 'I'm sure your dad was devastated too. I'm sure he did love you. Still does.'

'Funny way of showing it.'

Her palm flattened against his chest, her voice thick with sadness. 'I'm so sorry.'

So this was how distraction from his reality had panned out. Delving even deeper into his past. So not what he'd hoped for.

He tried to lighten the moment. 'Sure, it's fine, Kara.'

'It is now, yes. Look at what you've achieved. Just look at you, Declan. A career most people could never hope for. Sisters who are so, so proud of you—and you of them. A farm that provides food and an income, a beautiful house. More… so much more than many people have, and all because of you.'

She curled into him, hugging him close, and he felt the weight inside his chest begin to lift.

'It *is* fine—it's better than fine.'

He nuzzled his face into her hair and just for a few moments he let himself believe it could be.

They lay down on the grass, listening to the eerie night sounds, the fresh country air whispering over them. The familiar smells of his home mingled with Kara's scent. Her heat pressed against him; her hair tickled his chin.

Awareness prickled through his veins.

'You know what I think?' she whispered.

He doubted it was anything like what was running through *his* mind. But a man could hope. 'No.'

'I think we say to hell with them. To hell with everything they made us feel, the disappointment and the hate.' She rolled on to him, straddling him. 'We should let it all go. We deserve better. Much, much better. We need to forget it and take something for ourselves. What do you say?'

She made it sound so easy.

The air around them shimmered and suddenly her mouth was very close. Her breasts rubbed against his chest and he could feel them pebbling as she leaned closer. Her scent enveloped him and he grew hard again in an instant. Very hard. He wanted to kiss that mouth, those breasts, to take her to the edge of oblivion. To do it again and again until neither of them had any memories apart from this, here. Now.

'You have any ideas?'

'Oh, Declan, yes. Yes, I do.'

And then she was kissing him—hungry, hot kisses that obliterated the anger and filled his heart with something else. Something much better indeed.

CHAPTER THIRTEEN

KARA KISSED HIM because she had to get the cruel image of a boy trying to save his family out of her head. His eyes were filled with a lifetime of shadows, of hate and regret and sorrow, and she wanted to erase that too. To smooth down his edges, to change the blackness into light. She kissed him because she wanted to feel something, to be wanted.

And because she wanted him.

She wanted Declan more than anything she'd ever wanted before.

Meshing her hands into his hair, she kissed him with everything she had, told him with that kiss just how much he had touched her heart. And he kissed her back with the same longing, the same promises, the same damned wanting that had fizzed around them since that ball.

He rolled her onto her back and kissed hot trails down her neck, stripped off her top and bra and exposed her nipples to the cooling air. But his heat warmed her, made her dizzy, until she just wanted more of him. And more.

When his palm cupped her breast she arched against him, shocked by the moan coming from her throat, by how much she ached to have him inside her. When his mouth clamped her nipple and a shiver of desire rolled down her spine she thought she could now definitely die happy.

'God, Kara, I want you so much. It's killing me.'

His voice was deep and hoarse, more a growl than words. His eyes had darkened, were fierce and glittering with a need that she knew was mirrored in her own pupils.

'Have me. Take me.'

'Kiss me,' he whispered.

And she did. Again and again. Until her mind was almost numb and her lips were swollen and sore yet still hungry for more.

Her hands met his chest and she dragged off his shirt, buttons popping and flying who cared where. Then she pressed against him, slick skin on skin, and a primal, feral need shuddered through her. Grass tickled her back and the stream played a gentle backing track to his breathing, his words.

'Now these. Off.' He pushed off her wellies. No, he tried to push one off but it got stuck, so he tore himself away from her, knelt and tugged again at the first one, then the other, toppling backwards on the riverbank. His roar echoed through the trees. Somewhere an owl hooted.

She couldn't help the laugh. He looked magnificent, biceps bulging, muscled chest puffed out as he stood above her. All sexed-up because of her. 'But, Declan, I thought you wanted me to leave my shoes on?'

'Don't be ridiculous. Crazy, beautiful woman. How can I get to your jeans if you leave them on?'

He knelt and slid his hand to her jeans button, then he inched them down over her legs. Slowly. Too damned slowly.

'Besides, those leprechauns do nothing for me...but those ruby-red shoes...' He groaned. 'Man, next time...'

He pressed kisses down her abdomen, making her inhale sharply, sending spasms of need pulsing through her.

'Next time you put those on.'

Next time. He wanted a next time and they hadn't even finished this time. Had barely started. And, God, she definitely didn't want it to end. 'Whatever you want.'

'Everything. I want it all, Kara.'

And she could tell just how much he wanted her as he pressed against her. She unzipped his jeans, shrugged them off and took hold of his erection, felt him harden even more, felt the heat surge through him, the shift in his breathing. Until it was almost impossible to breathe herself for needing him inside her.

'Declan, now, please. I need you. *Now.*'

His fingers roamed her thighs, opened her legs and then he was sheathed and over her, entering her, pressing deep and hard. And there was nothing then except the sheer power of this man and this never-ending need.

'Kara. Kara. My God, you are so beautiful.'

Her name on his lips was like music. His mouth was against her cheek, against her ear, in her hair with every wonderful thrust. Hard at first, frantic, desperate until she was so close…so close. Then he slowed the rhythm and looked at her, holding back as the pressure inside her, outside her, over her, started to increase. Slowly, too slowly, not slowly enough, he kissed her with such need, such passion, that nothing else mattered. Nothing but this.

'Declan... I... I...'

'I know... I know...'

She was on the edge and that fired something urgent in him. Declan shifted her hips as he felt her clamp around him, drove deeper inside her, wanting to savour every moment, to ride sensation after sensation. Her hair pooled over the grass. Her body arched as he held her waist and rocked her.

But he held back. It would be too easy to let loose and put his own pleasure first. He wanted to show her that not all men were like her husband and his father—that there were good men too, who would put her needs first. This was for Kara—for everything she'd had to endure.

He put all thoughts of consequences to one side. He didn't know what would happen next—couldn't promise her more than this. Didn't know anything past this moment. He wanted it to last forever, but he was riding an edge and it wouldn't take much to plunge him over.

He slanted his mouth across hers, tasted her again, ran his hands along the smooth soft shape of her curves, gripped her bottom and pressed deeper.

'Declan…' She was panting now, her head rocking back. 'God, yes.'

And he tried to hold on just a moment longer, clasping her close, stroking her hair, looking into those deep emerald eyes misty with satisfaction. But when her hands gripped his back and she pulled him closer, moving her body in perfect rhythm as she moaned deep and long and loud, he was lost. And only Kara could show him the way back.

'So, will you give me a ride back to uni or not?' Roisin grabbed a rosy apple from the bowl on the kitchen benchtop and bit down hard. 'Only I can go with Ronan and he's leaving in a few minutes. Tell me now.'

'Don't be so rude. I'm sure Declan will offer when he's ready.' Niamh smiled at Kara and rolled her eyes. Then winced as she dodged a face full of porridge from Declan Junior's well-aimed spoon. It landed next to Kara on the table with a plop. 'Nice try, sonny. Next time see if you can get your evil Auntie Roisin square on the nose.'

The little boy grinned and loaded his spoon. Kara could see the glint in his eye. Like uncle, like nephew. It seemed the Underwood genes ran deep.

'Nah-ah. Only joking.' This time Niamh made sure the food went where it was supposed to. Then she lowered her voice. 'I can't thank you enough for bringing him over. The first time he brings home a girl...and, well, I'm so glad it was you. Don't be too long coming back again. Any nonsense from His Lordship over there and you get on to me, d'you hear? He might be my older brother but I'm not averse to kicking his bu—' She picked up a large bowl and smiled sweetly to the rest of the family. 'Now, who wants the rest of these eggs?'

Sunday morning and everyone had gathered for yet another meal. The scent of sausages and bacon had drawn Kara from the cottage, but she didn't feel hungry. After a sleepless night she didn't feel anything at all except numb, and yet at the same time overwhelmed.

She'd fooled herself into believing just for a few moments that making love with Declan wouldn't carve a piece of him onto her heart, wouldn't matter.

It did.

His story had touched her. His passion and determination had lit something deep in her. She hadn't just got a slice of him in her heart—she had a gaping hole filled with him.

This wasn't a juvenile infatuation or some kind of wishful thinking. She loved him. In such a short, intense space of time she'd fallen completely for a player who, underneath it all, wasn't a player at all.

He was a man trying hard to carve himself some space in a life that was full, trying to squeeze some joy from a life that had been tarnished.

She loved him. The realisation hit her square in the chest as she heard his laughter and turned instinctively towards it with a leap in her heart.

She loved him, and instead of being the joyous thing Briana believed in it was terrifying. To lose control of her feelings—to put herself there again. The one thing Kara had tried so hard never to allow to happen.

Swallowing back the ache, she turned away.

'Are you ready?' Declan called to her from under a spaghetti of chubby arms and legs and a lot of giggling.

She wanted to run away, far away, and yet she'd never be ready to leave this. For the first time ever she felt as if she truly belonged somewhere, and knowing she'd never come back was breaking her in two. 'Give me a few minutes to get my things sorted. I won't be long.'

'Okay, well, I'll go with Ronan, then. Finally I get an answer I can understand.' Roisin sighed. 'Lovely to meet you, Kara. Please keep doing whatever it is you're doing to Declan…it suits him. He's actually nice.'

His sister wrapped her into a big warm hug and Kara squeezed her eyes shut.

'And come back soon.'

She couldn't keep doing this. 'Bye, Roisin. Keep up with those studies. If ever you get the chance to come over to London I'd love to show you around.'

'That would be great. I'd love to. You can count on it.'

And then she was gone, along with Ronan. A thick weight pressed in Kara's chest. Two down, another dozen or so goodbyes to go.

Somehow she managed to get a few moments alone in her bedroom to pack away her things and take stock. Although she'd been taking stock for hours—and it had got her precisely nowhere. No matter how much she tried to fill her lungs with fresh country air she still had trouble breathing.

She could not let Declan know her true feelings and she certainly didn't know his—couldn't guess. She couldn't turn a weekend into something more. Couldn't expect him to invest the same kind of emotion she'd foolishly invested.

And besides—they were colleagues. He was her boss and they'd crossed a line. What the hell had they been thinking? She couldn't love him. But she did.

'Time to go, Kara. Give me your bag and I'll put it in the car.'

He was standing in the doorway, but he didn't come in and kiss her as she'd thought he might.

He just gave her a faint smile, then turned to wait for her, avoiding eye contact.

Last night they'd stumbled back up the hill sati-ated and exhilarated. Stopping to kiss every few steps until it had taken an age to get home. He'd cuddled against her in bed and they'd made love again. Then at some point in the night she'd fallen into a feverish sleep. And into regret.

Not regret that she'd slept with him, but that she couldn't…wouldn't…shouldn't do it again.

Now he was decidedly distant. Did he think it had been a mistake too? Was he struggling with *what next*?

It would be so easy to carry on as if everything would be fine. To pretend everything *could* be fine. But she was tired of pretending now. She just wanted to go home. Alone.

'Declan. We need to talk…about us.'

He put his finger against her lips and shook his head. 'Not here, Kara. Not now. We have to go. Everyone's waiting to say goodbye.'

Including him, it would seem.

'Okay. Then let's do it.' With a sigh she closed the door behind her and followed him to the leaving committee, that ache in her chest intensifying.

The hardest goodbye was Mary's. Surrounded by the little ones, Declan's mother wiped away a tear. 'So grand to have you here, Kara, my love. You must come back and visit us soon.'

'I'll try.'

'And I think I might come over to see you and that grand clinic you have.' She touched her damaged cheek. 'Who knows what you could do to make things a little better, right? I think it's time.'

Kara watched with a heavy heart as Mary hugged her son. How long would it be until he came back again? And who would he bring next time? No—she wouldn't allow herself to think that. Couldn't imagine standing back and letting someone else love him. This was, she knew, special…for them both. And very special for Mary. Two women loving one man.

But was it harder to be his mother and have him gone from her day-to-day life, but to be tied to him for ever? Or to be Kara—to have him gone from her life but to see him every day?

Fighting back tears, she settled into the car en route to Dublin. The grey road stretched out ahead and the sky was black with rain over fields that seemed to have changed from lush green to brown overnight. She didn't know what to say, even where to begin.

So she stuck to the mundane, her throat too full of goodbyes to start another. 'Looks like the weather's changed for the worse.'

'They say if you don't like the weather here, just wait five minutes. It's fickle like that.' He shrugged and looked ahead, retreating further and further into whatever black mood he'd created.

She couldn't bear the thought of this kind of pointless half-hearted small talk and shopping and sightseeing and more pretending for the next few hours. 'Declan, I don't think I can face shopping.'

'Okay.'

He glanced across to her, hands white on the steering wheel, his jaw tight. She wanted to hug him close, to look forward to a future with him in it—at work and at home. In a house like his. She wanted to rewind to last night, wanted him to kiss her again and tell her she was marvellous. But mostly, she wanted not to have fallen in love with him at all.

'Shall I see if we can get an earlier flight?'

'Yes. Yes, that would be good, I think. All things considered.' Not marvellous at all. Not even a bit.

His eyes narrowed—and was that a flicker of relief there too? Her heart began to break. There really was no going back.

'Okay. If that's what you want.'

'Yes. Yes, it is.'

So instead of finding the *craic* in Dublin's fair city and seeing the splendour of Trinity College they landed in a cold and dreary Heathrow in the early afternoon. The crowds pressed in as they jostled through Arrivals and all she wanted to do was get home to her apartment and pull her sheets over her head—like Safia had—and shut the world out.

As the underground train rattled towards the city Declan turned to her, his eyes clouded, voice flat. 'Thanks very much for helping me out this weekend. You were amazing. I hope you didn't hate it too much.'

Helping him out. Was that all it was, in the end? Yes. It was. And she'd been under no illusions—apart from her own.

That damned lump was back in her throat again. 'No, it was wonderful. Thanks for inviting me.'

'You know…it was amazing. Really, the best.'

But… There was a but. There had to be a but.

He hesitated. His face closed in and she thought for a moment he was going to kiss her, but he played with a lock of her hair instead, running it through his fingers, back and forth. Judging by his frown a battle was being fought in his head. She didn't know what or who was going to be the winner but she had a bad feeling it wouldn't be her.

And it was so hard for her to stay quiet…because she always spoke first and regretted it afterwards—but this time, *this time*, she knew it was better to keep her mouth shut and her emotions hidden.

His mouth kicked up at one side. 'But we did agree… You know what it's like in London—so busy, work's full-on…neither of us has time for a relationship.'

He was right of course. She'd trodden that path before and all she'd achieved was misery and regret for all involved. Sometimes loving someone just wasn't enough. The pain in her chest tightened.

'I know what we agreed, Declan. No strings. And that's fine. Actually, that's great. Perfect. That suits me down to the ground. Because, as I said, I don't want anything to interfere with my job.' She forced a smile and fought the tears. She would not show him how she felt. 'Back to normal, then. I'll see you in the morning, bright and early.'

'Not quite.' He looked at his feet. 'I just got a text message from Leo. Karen's mum's well enough to be left, so Karen's keen to get back to work. You've been reallocated back to your old team. From tomorrow.'

And he'd had to tell her this on a busy train? A sharp fist wedged under her ribcage. There really were no ties at all. Or the man was a damned sight better at acting than she was.

The train screeched to a halt. She glanced up. The next stop was hers. Biting down on her bottom lip, she tried to keep her voice light. 'Okay, well, this is it, then.'

'I'll see you back to your flat.' He picked up her bag.

'No. No, you won't.' She took her bag back from him, being careful not brush against him or inhale any of his scent that drove her wild. Better to say goodbye now, here on a busy train, than on her doorstep, watching him walk away and wishing him back.

At least this way she could be the one to leave and keep some semblance of dignity. Fighting tears, she forced her mouth into a smile. What she didn't want to do was rip open their...relationship...and tear it to shreds, into tiny heart-breaking pieces.

What she wanted to do was throttle him instead—and herself—for letting it get this far. For making love, for allowing herself to fall in love with him.

'I think I'm better going home on my own.'

His nostrils flared. 'I'm coming with you. No arguing. You could get mugged, or attacked, or anything.'

'And you think that risk bothers me?' She could deal with a mugger better than a broken heart any day. 'Declan, leave it. I'm not one of your sisters. You can't tell me what to do, and you can't dictate what happens in my life. I'm going home on my own.'

'But why?' He shook his head as if finally realising this was the end. 'Wait—'

'No, Declan. This is my stop. I have to go. I can't spend the day going up and down the Central Line.' Or round and round in circles, getting nowhere.

A screech of brakes and a judder. The doors swished open and a rush of hot thick air entered the carriage.

His hand was on her shoulder. 'I'm sorry, Kara.'

'Look, we both knew this weekend was a one-off. What happens in Ireland stays in Ireland, right?'

Her fist tightened around her bag's strap and she concentrated on not letting her voice crack. She could not give in to her emotions. Later, maybe, when she was alone. But not now. Definitely not now.

'Really, there's nothing to be sorry about. We both knew what we were getting ourselves into.'

He lifted his eyes to hers and she saw someone struggling with a host of demons. And losing.

'Did we?'

* * *

Damn. Declan kicked the tube station wall and relished the pain emanating from his foot, let the hurt stoke his raging heartbeat. Then he kicked with the other one, just for the hell of it.

In the distance Kara walked down the platform to the escalator, back straight, shoulders taut, hair skimming her coat in a river of blonde curls. Curls he wanted to lose himself in. Hair he wanted to be pooling over the sheets on his bed. *Their bed.* In a future that was filled with her laughter and her sparkling eyes, her forthright honesty.

A few weeks ago he'd been satisfied with the life he'd carved for himself. Relationships that cost little more than his credit card bill. Work that he could invest as much of himself in as he physically and mentally was able. A job he loved. Now his life was brimful of complications every which way he turned. And he didn't know what the hell to do about it.

How could he let himself fall in love?

His heart twisted some more. *Did* he love her? *Could* he love her? The idea was so out there that he couldn't reconcile it. For a man who didn't

.lieve in love the idea was laughable. But what else could describe the chaos in his heart?

Lust. He thought about how his body reacted to her. That was what it was. Lust.

And it was foolish even to want that. The way she'd been behaving all day—so closed-off and quiet—he'd got the message that she'd thought the whole weekend had been a stupid mistake. At least, making love had been a mistake—because that marked the point where everything had changed between them. Become harder, stronger, deeper.

Or was it that she was hiding her true feelings? Because the devastation in her eyes wasn't just at saying goodbye to his family, that much he knew.

He watched as she rose on the escalator, her red suede boots eventually disappearing out of view, and fought the urge to run after her. His heart splintered.

He'd managed just fine on his own until now—always setting the rules, always being the giver. He didn't know how to take something for himself, to rewrite the rulebook. He'd never allowed himself to get in so deep that he'd felt helpless, confused. So goddamn out of control.

Watching her leave was a million times worse than watching his father turn his back on his family. This time he didn't shout and plead. This time he let her go. Because, after all, that was the right thing to do. Before it got too deep and hurt too much.

She'd think he was mad enough having got off at her tube station just to watch her walk away, never mind chasing her down to have a conversation which started and ended with, *I can't. I don't know how. I don't want to love you.*

Because loving her would be too hard. Too easy. Too much.

But, God, he wanted her. The pain in his chest settled into a keen ache. As he picked up his bag and waited for the next train home he exhaled. Tried to shake the headache settling on his forehead. But it hung around, making his brain a hot mess of fuzz. He wanted her, but he couldn't take a risk on having her. He wasn't going to let anyone tread on his heart.

The harsh truth was, the weekend hadn't been a mistake. Falling for her had.

CHAPTER FOURTEEN

DRAKE'S WAS BUZZING. Sadly, Kara wasn't. But for the sake of the team she tried very hard to be. And apparently she was failing.

'Are you okay, Kara?' Angela, the surgical reg, put down a fresh glass of Pinot Noir and squeezed in next to her at the crowded dark wooden table. 'Only, you've been quiet for a long time. And that's just not normal. For you, anyway.'

'I'm fine. Really. Sorry, I've just had a lot on my mind recently.' Declan mainly. Well, Declan totally.

Kara laughed, wishing she'd managed to mask her feelings more successfully. Even during her brief social visits to Safia the girl had been asking awkward questions and raising those dark eyebrows, muttering something about losing the love of your life.

And she had.

Those few weeks with Declan had been the

most precious and amazing time of her life. He'd fired something in her. Made her want things out of reach, want the impossible. Allowed her to dream. And now it was gone and she felt bereft all over again, as if something had been physically wrenched from her, and it hurt like hell.

She knew it would take time—but she would eventually heal. She just hadn't thought it would hurt so much. Working long hours on little sleep was stretching her to her limit, but whenever she closed her eyes she saw his face, heard his voice.

No longer. She was through with this. At least she was going to try to be through with it until she really was.

'You know what, Ange? I've decided to hell with it. I'm going to stop looking backwards and start again.'

Again. How many times was she going to start again?

This was definitely the last time. Over the past two weeks she'd fluctuated between *damn the man* and checking her phone to make sure it was still functioning as she prayed for a call from him. For anything. A glimpse of him—something. But he'd been strangely elusive.

So it turned out he didn't want her after all.

And so she'd consigned herself to being just another of his conquests.

Her stomach knotted at what they'd lost.

Inhaling deeply, she drained her wineglass and put it down. No point in wallowing in self-pity. She had a wonderful job, and so much to give to her patients and her career.

Despite everything she'd found a different place to belong—here, at work, doing surgery, saving lives. And while it didn't fulfil every need it kept her busy and rewarded enough not to dwell too much on what might have been. She had a great career path and a supportive team.

'Well, thanks for the drink, everyone. I'm going to head off now. It's been a very long day.'

Tomorrow was the first day of the rest of her life, and she was going to make the most of every second. Declan Underwood be damned.

Declan assisted the Kate's emergency room staff to lift the badly burnt young man across from the paramedics' trolley to the department's one.

'Cause of the fire?' Declan always liked to know exactly what he was dealing with.

contacted her for two weeks. Why he'd avoided looking for those emerald eyes and skyscraper heels in Drake's Bar or the staffroom or the hospital corridors. Why he hadn't listened out for her laugh. And why he'd been unable to sleep.

Because he had no idea what he was dealing with. But he had a nasty suspicion that it was a lot more than lust.

After settling the stable-for-now John Doe in the intensive care unit he made his way up to the private wing and went to see someone else it was going to be hard to say goodbye to. No matter how much he tried not to get involved, he couldn't help himself.

'Well, well. Look at you now. All ready to go?'

Safia stood in her home country's ornate dress, surrounded by packed suitcases, and smiled her regal smile. A genuine but nervous one. 'Yes. Thank you, Dec. But it feels a bit weird, going out there into the big wide world. Everyone wants to see the scarred Sheikha.'

'You will be fine. You *are* fine—just look at you.' He checked the reddened skin on her face, knowing that over time she would have minimal scarring. 'Give it a few months until everything has settled down and I'm sure you'll feel better about the results. And make sure you do the physio and attend all my follow-up appointments.' He gave her a pretend frown. 'Because I *will* growl if I have to.'

She waved a hand at him. 'You mean like you have for the past couple of weeks?'

'I have not.'

'Mr Underwood, you have been acting more like my dad than the chilled-out cool guy you were when I first came in here.'

She tapped her fingers on the bedside table and he marvelled at the flexibility she had there now, in such a short space of time.

'Missing someone?'

'No.'

'You forget that I might be a princess but I'm also a teenager. And I have to lie a lot to manage being both.' She shook her head and rolled her eyes. 'That looked a lot like lying.'

So what if he had been lying? There was no point discussing his private life—er…his nonexistent private life—with a young girl. She was seventeen. What the heck did she know about life or love? But then at thirty years of age what did he? Absolutely nothing, it seemed.

He might as well be talking to one of his sisters. Hell, he was surrounded by women who thought they knew better about his love-life than he did.

'No, I'm just trying to do my job, Safia. Just getting on with things. I like to be busy.'

Her eyes glinted suspiciously. 'That's exactly what she said too.'

'You've seen her?' His heart did a clumsy jitter.

He didn't need to ask who Safia was talking about. He'd had ample opportunity to see Kara too, just hadn't taken it. He'd needed time and space.

And that hadn't worked either.

'She popped by yesterday to say goodbye and wish me well.' Safia frowned. 'She looked about as happy as you do. And she tried to pretend she was fine too, but she had all the classic symptoms.'

'Symptoms?' Now his heart did a double jitter. What was wrong with her? 'Symptoms of what?'

'In here.' Safia pointed to *BFF!* magazine's front page. *'"How to Know You're Falling In Love: 20 Classic Signs."'* She flicked open the mag and ran her finger down a page. '"*Loss of appetite.*" She refused a chocolate when I offered it to her. And no doctor refuses chocolates. Ever. "*Sleeplessness.*" She had big dark circles under her eyes. She looked exhausted and her hands were shaky. "*Lack of concentration.*" She kept checking her phone and really didn't have a lot to say…'

'Okay—I don't want to be rude…'

Declan relaxed. The girl was talking about a little dream world she'd created to pass the time while she'd been in hospital. Fair play to her too—whatever helped the healing process was fine by him. But what he'd shared with Kara wasn't the stuff of teenage magazines. It had been very adult. Very intense. Amazing. Life-changing.

And he'd been a damned fool to let her go. But he just didn't know how to get her back. Or even if she would be interested.

'*Perfect,*' she'd said as he'd flailed around for words. '*What happens in Ireland stays in Ireland.*'

'But I don't think—'

Safia held up her hand. She was going to make

a very fine wife to any sheikh brave enough to take her on.

'And when I asked her if she was missing someone, she lied too.'

'Safi…seriously….'

'I *am* being serious. Love is a serious matter—especially when you don't admit it. And it makes you grumpy.' She shrugged apologetically. 'Stop frowning. I'm just trying to be strong for you until you can be strong yourself. Everyone needs someone to help them along. Right?'

He hadn't seen that coming. Why were some people just so damned…*right*?

His heart did a little leap. 'And she lied too?'

'Yes. I think she loves you just as much as you love her. I didn't think you were that stupid, Mr Underwood.'

Stupid. Yes. *Eejit.* Yes. He resisted checking the magazine's list for the other signs of falling in love, because if he was honest he knew them well enough by now. He couldn't think of anything else but her. His mouth ached to talk to her, to kiss her. His arms cried out to hold her. His feet wanted to take off in their own direction to find her. His whole body had a physical withdrawal. And don't even ask about his brain…

So, yes. He'd fallen in love with her. And the only pain that love had caused was this—this not accepting it, this fighting it. Not being able to tell her. To cherish her. To hold her. See her. He'd been so scared to feel it. Admit it.

What the hell he was going to do about it, though, he couldn't fathom. He'd let something precious slip through his fingers while he'd been so damned focused on why they couldn't be together.

He missed Kara like he'd miss oxygen. He missed her crazy attitude and her smile. He missed her scent and her heat. He missed that she knew what he needed even before he did.

And if he was going to manage living a life here in London he wanted her to be in it. Somehow. In fact he couldn't imagine another day without her. He just had to work out what to do about it.

Kara reached the top of the steps to her apartment and fitted the key into her lock. Looking back to the pavement below, she remembered the time Declan had dropped her off on his bike and the kiss they'd shared. Good times. Special times. Even now her skin prickled with awareness at the thought. Like some sort of sixth sense. He'd always had that effect on her—as if her body just knew when he was near.

In the distance she heard the distant purr of a motorbike. Her heart stalled as the awareness intensified.

Don't be silly. There are plenty of motorbikes in London. For goodness' sake, she couldn't keep having that reaction to every motorbike sound. She'd be exhausted.

Kick-starting her foolish heart again, she turned the key and put one foot inside her apartment. The purr turned into a deep, throaty roar. Louder and louder.

It was the kind of roar that only one type of bike made—the kind of roar you recognised. Her stomach clenched.

Could it be?

Sure enough, at the end of the road she watched a shiny black and chrome bike turn the corner, then pull up at the kerb, with a rider who would not look out of place on the cover of a magazine. Suddenly there didn't seem to be enough air to fill her lungs. When she did manage to inhale her breath was stuttering and sharp. Clutching her handbag strap, she felt her hand shake.

Dressed in black jeans and the old leather jacket that had definitely seen better days, but which she loved almost as much as the rider because it had saved his life, Declan looked dangerous and edgy. Far from his usual cool exterior. His eyes flashed with apprehension; a muscle twitched in his jaw. He didn't smile.

What was he here for? Her mouth dropped open. She put a hand to it and resisted the temptation to run down the steps and throw her arms round his neck.

Instead of speaking he climbed the steps, put a finger to her lips and shook his head, closing off all conversation. Then he walked her to the pavement, pulled out a helmet from the top box and fastened it under her chin. His eyes glanced to her legs, to her ruby-red shoes. A flicker of heat warmed the apprehension.

As she climbed onto the back of the bike he took her hand and steadied her as he'd done before. A flash of electricity buzzed between them, making the hairs on her arms stand upright. It would never diminish, it seemed, this attraction, this connection. Even when her heart was broken, when her head knew things could never work out, some parts of her body just would not give up on him.

She wanted to ask him where the hell they were going. What he was doing there so late at night. She wanted to believe this was what she hoped it might be. But as she slid her arms around the body she now knew so well and had ached so much to touch she reminded herself that this was not going to be what she wanted. That she must try to stay detached... But how could she when she was glued to him on a powerful motorbike?

There must be an emergency, a problem, something serious to do with work, his family. Because why else would he be here?

Resting her head against his back, she clung on to that thought as they sped through the dark streets of London. Faster and faster they flew, the cool autumn wind blowing her hair around her face. And still she didn't know where they were headed, or why. But she knew that for these few minutes she would hold on to some kind of hope.

Soon enough they reached the riverbank. Now, in the dark, it had a different feel to it. Down in the houseboats someone was playing a slow soft tune as yellow lights danced across the water. Different, but equally beautiful. Like Declan. He'd changed. Thinner, maybe. His cheeks had hollowed out a little, making his cheekbones even more sleek and sharp. Guarded, but alert, his eyes danced along with the lights.

He lifted her off the bike and threw his helmet onto the grass. Then he pulled hers off too and his hands were cupping her face, in her hair, pulling her closer until his lips met hers and she couldn't help but melt into his kiss.

So it was indeed something serious. At his touch her body went into overdrive. She'd missed this so much. Missed this closeness, his smell. He tasted of fresh air. Of love. Of a future.

She'd been there before. It had failed spectacularly.

Her heart beat loud and slow against her ribcage. She put her hands on his chest and pulled

away. 'Stop…stop. We can't do this. I'm sorry. I
need to go. *We* need to go.'

'No…I have to tell you something.'

He walked her along the path where the scent of
sweet aniseed herbs filled the air. Around them
the breeze dropped, as did the music. And as they
left the busyness behind it felt as if they were the
only two people in this city of eight million.

He stopped and turned to face her. 'I've been
a prize idiot, Kara. I let you walk away from me
and I know I shouldn't have. I really should have
told you how I felt.'

Her heart seized at his words. Part ecstasy, part
regret. 'In what way? *Felt*?'

'Feel. How I *feel* about you. I was hurt badly
when my dad left, and I saw what love can do to
a person when it isn't returned. It can eat away at
every part of you. Can make you mistrust, make
you question yourself, your worth. It stripped
away my ability to risk loving someone else. So
I tried hard not to care. I used it all as an excuse
not to get involved and give any part of myself
away and it worked fine for years.'

'I know.'

'But then I met you and everything changed. My life changed. And the lives of those around me.'

He stepped back and gave her a cautious smile that reached to the bottom of her heart and spread to every corner.

'I love you, Kara. More than anything. And I want some kind of a future with you—'

'Shh. Stop. I can't.' There—she'd said it. 'I just can't.' Then she turned and stumbled across the grass, headed who knew where, blinking back tears. Why had she let him bring her here to say these things only to break her heart a little more? 'Just go and find someone else to fall in love with, okay? Because I can't do this.'

'Hey, we can do anything we want.' He tugged her arm and pulled her round, seriousness etched across his face. 'I know you're scared. Hell, I am too. I've never done this before…and I know I'm making a huge mess of it right now. But it's from my heart, Kara. We can work things out together. Just the two of us. We can carve our own space. We belong together.'

'No. I can't, Declan.' Her heart shattering, she dragged her wrists from his hands. *Belong?* How much had she ached for that all her life? And now she'd found it, it was beyond her grasp. 'I'm so scared things will change. That we'll get all wrapped up in this bit and not see the end hit us. I couldn't bear it if you fell out of love with me. If I'm not enough for you.'

'You don't think you're enough?' He tipped back his head and laughed. 'Kara, you're more than enough for any man. And certainly perfect for me.' He was reaching into his jacket pocket now. 'Is that why you retreated that day we left my mam's?'

'Because I fell in love with you, Declan. Despite how much I tried not to. You and your damned lovely family won me over. I didn't know what to do after we'd made love. I was so confused. It changed everything—it changed my heart.'

She touched her chest and felt her heart beating a crazy rhythm. Fast and shallow.

'But we'd both agreed there couldn't be more. And you didn't exactly make me feel like you *wanted* more. I don't want to say yes if it'll end in a few years. I can't take that risk. I can't do that again. Not with you. I love you too much.'

He palmed her cheek with his hand and looked

deep into her eyes. Never had she seen such passion. True. Stark. Raw.

'Oh, my God, Kara, you think that if something doesn't work I'll chuck it aside? Get a replacement wife and family? If I promise you one thing it is this—I will be there for you, whatever happens. To love and cherish. In sickness and health. Those vows mean something to me too. I am not my father.'

'No. No, you're not.'

When he hadn't contacted her she'd branded him with the same attributes her husband had had: shallow and selfish. But Declan wasn't like that. He'd shown loyalty and belief and strength to everyone around him. And now he was offering that to her too. It had taken him a bit longer than she'd hoped. But he'd done it. And she didn't doubt his sincerity now. Or his love. Because she could see that in his smile, in his eyes.

'Right now I have something to ask you.' He lowered one knee onto the grass and pulled out a small box, revealing a stunning emerald ring. 'Kara, I love you with all my heart. I don't want to imagine another day without you in my life. Would you do me the honour of being my wife?'

'Oh, my God. *Oh, my God.* That is beautiful.'

Tears pricked her eyes. She pressed her hand against her mouth to stop her lips from wobbling but she couldn't. Couldn't breathe or speak. He loved her. *Her.* And she loved him right back.

'It was my grandmother's. One of the only things we salvaged from the fire. I want you to have it. Mammy wants you to have it. Naimh says she'll kill you if you don't. The whole damned clan want— You get the picture. Please say yes. Or I'll be in a whole lot of bother.'

'Say it again.'

'What?'

'The whole proposal thing...' Her throat ached. 'I just love that accent. It makes my heart go diddly-diddly. Go on, say it again...please.'

He shook his head and rolled his eyes, but he wasn't angry. He was happy. Very happy indeed. 'Kara, I love you with all my—'

Stamping her feet and clapping, she squeaked, tugging at his shoulder. It seemed that once the right someone came along you knew. You just *knew.* 'Yes! Yes! I will marry you. Yes! Now, get up and come here.'

'Aww. Give me a minute...'

His hand was on her ankle, his fingers running tiny circles around her foot, up her leg. Heat shot through her as he found that point…yes, *there*… that made her shiver with need.

'Now, these are very fine shoes. How about we take a very quick drive home so I can spend a little time getting to know them…?'

'You want me to definitely leave them on this time?'

'Hell, yes.'

She knelt down next to him, looking forward to getting to know him a lot better too. As he smiled at her she reached out and touched his beautiful face, ran her finger down his cheek until it met his mouth.

Then she leaned in close and whispered, *'Kiss me.'*

* * * * *

MILLS & BOON®
Large Print Medical

February

TEMPTED BY HER BOSS	Scarlet Wilson
HIS GIRL FROM NOWHERE	Tina Beckett
FALLING FOR DR DIMITRIOU	Anne Fraser
RETURN OF DR IRRESISTIBLE	Amalie Berlin
DARING TO DATE HER BOSS	Joanna Neil
A DOCTOR TO HEAL HER HEART	Annie Claydon

March

A SECRET SHARED...	Marion Lennox
FLIRTING WITH THE DOC OF HER DREAMS	Janice Lynn
THE DOCTOR WHO MADE HER LOVE AGAIN	Susan Carlisle
THE MAVERICK WHO RULED HER HEART	Susan Carlisle
AFTER ONE FORBIDDEN NIGHT...	Amber McKenzie
DR PERFECT ON HER DOORSTEP	Lucy Clark

April

IT STARTED WITH NO STRINGS...	Kate Hardy
ONE MORE NIGHT WITH HER DESERT PRINCE...	Jennifer Taylor
FLIRTING WITH DR OFF-LIMITS	Robin Gianna
FROM FLING TO FOREVER	Avril Tremayne
DARE SHE DATE AGAIN?	Amy Ruttan
THE SURGEON'S CHRISTMAS WISH	Annie O'Neil

MILLS & BOON®
Large Print Medical

May

PLAYING THE PLAYBOY'S SWEETHEART	Carol Marinelli
UNWRAPPING HER ITALIAN DOC	Carol Marinelli
A DOCTOR BY DAY...	Emily Forbes
TAMED BY THE RENEGADE	Emily Forbes
A LITTLE CHRISTMAS MAGIC	Alison Roberts
CHRISTMAS WITH THE MAVERICK MILLIONAIRE	Scarlet Wilson

June

MIDWIFE'S CHRISTMAS PROPOSAL	Fiona McArthur
MIDWIFE'S MISTLETOE BABY	Fiona McArthur
A BABY ON HER CHRISTMAS LIST	Louisa George
A FAMILY THIS CHRISTMAS	Sue MacKay
FALLING FOR DR DECEMBER	Susanne Hampton
SNOWBOUND WITH THE SURGEON	Annie Claydon

July

HOW TO FIND A MAN IN FIVE DATES	Tina Beckett
BREAKING HER NO-DATING RULE	Amalie Berlin
IT HAPPENED ONE NIGHT SHIFT	Amy Andrews
TAMED BY HER ARMY DOC'S TOUCH	Lucy Ryder
A CHILD TO BIND THEM	Lucy Clark
THE BABY THAT CHANGED HER LIFE	Louisa Heaton